MARRIED
FOR THEIR
MIRACLE BABY

MARRIED FOR THEIR MIRACLE BABY

BY

SORAYA LANE

First published in Great Britain 2016
By Mills & Boon, an imprint of HarperCollins*Publishers*
1 London Bridge Street, London, SE1 9GF

Large Print edition 2016

© 2016 Soraya Lane

ISBN: 978-0-263-26216-2

C463791368

Printed and bound in Great Britain
by CPI Antony Rowe, Chippenham, Wiltshire

For my mother, Maureen.
Thank you for everything.

CHAPTER ONE

BLAKE GOLDSMITH TOOK a slow sip of whiskey, enjoying the burn of the straight liquor as he swallowed. He wasn't a big drinker, but he'd fast developed a taste for whiskey on the rocks to help get him through the torturous task of attending cocktail parties and gala events. He gazed down at the ice sitting forlorn in the glass. *Darn.* He either had to go without or brave the crowd mingling near the bar again. Neither option appealed to him right now.

Instead he decided to stretch his legs and head outside. If anyone stopped him, he could blame his departure on needing some fresh air. As soon as the auction was over, he was heading home anyway. He craved the solitude of flying, the closeness of being with his unit when he was serving. If he had half the chance, he'd be high-tailing it to wherever they were stationed and not coming back. *If only that were an option.*

"Excuse me," he muttered, touching a woman's elbow as he passed, eyes downcast so he didn't have to engage.

After a while, everyone started to look the same—a sea of black tuxedos and white shirts mixed with elegant women in sparkly dresses. He should have been used to it by now, but playing the black sheep turned good wasn't a part he'd ever wanted, and neither was being part of glittering society parties.

Wow. Blake squared his shoulders, stood a little straighter as he stared across the room. She was standing alone, back to the large windows that overlooked a twinkling New York City below. Her dark red hair was loose and falling over her shoulders, lipstick bright in contrast to her pale skin. She was like a perfectly formed doll, her posture perfect, one hand holding a full glass of champagne, the other clasping a tiny purse. In a room where all the women were starting to look scarily similar with their perfectly coiffed updos and black dresses, she was like the breath of fresh air he'd been so desperately craving only moments before.

Blake didn't waste time. She was alone, which meant she was either waiting for her date to return or actually solo. Either way, he wanted to get to her before anyone else did. He might be avoiding the pressure to settle down, but introducing himself to a beautiful woman would make the night a whole lot more interesting.

He excused himself past a few more people, striding across the room, eyes locked on her. *So much for a boring night out to buy some art and make the company look good.* His evening was looking better by the second. Blake cleared his throat and smiled when dark brown eyes met his.

"I'd ask if you want another drink, but it doesn't look like you've even touched this one," he said. "Unless you don't like champagne."

The redhead laughed, tipping back a little so her hair tumbled over her shoulders, the unblemished skin of her neck on show. "I love champagne. I'm just…"

Blake laughed. "Bored?"

She grimaced, and it only made him like her more. "Yeah," she said softly. "You could say that."

"I'm Blake," he said, holding out a hand. "Blake Goldsmith."

She reached hers out and he shook it, her skin warm against his. "Saffron Wells."

"So what's a girl like you doing here alone?"

"A bored girl?" she asked.

Blake raised an eyebrow. "No, a beautiful one."

Her smile was sweet. "I promised a friend I'd come, but it's not really my thing." Saffron shrugged. "She's an artist—one of her pieces is being auctioned tonight, so I couldn't really say no. Besides, I don't get out much."

She might feel out of place, but she sure

looked the part, as if it was exactly her scene. Blake glanced down when she looked away, eyes traveling over her blue satin dress, admiring her legs. It was short and strapless, and it took every inch of his willpower to stop staring. She was a knockout.

"So what do you do?" he asked.

"I'm having some time out right now," she replied, her smile fading. "I'm just making coffee and…"

Blake cringed, wishing he'd asked something less invasive. He hadn't wanted to put her on the spot or make her uncomfortable. "I love coffee. The barista at my local café is my favorite person in the world."

"How about you?" she asked.

Now Blake was really regretting his line of questioning. He'd walked straight into that one. "Family business. I'm here tonight because no one else would take my place."

"Poor you."

"Yeah, something like that." Blake hated talking about himself, and he liked the fact that this beautiful woman seemed to have no idea who he was. If he read another tabloid or blog article about his most-eligible-bachelor status, he'd lose it. And the lies surrounding his dad's death were driving him to drink. So to chat with a woman like Saffron and not deal with any of that was refreshing to say the least.

A waiter passed and Blake held up a hand, beckoning him over. He smiled and placed his empty whiskey glass on the tray, taking a champagne and putting it into Saffron's hand. He removed her other one, ignoring the look of protest on her face, and then he took another glass for himself.

"I was perfectly happy nursing that," she said.

"Nothing worse than warm champagne," Blake told her. "Want to get some fresh air?"

Saffron's smile was small, but it was there. "Sure. Any excuse to get out of here."

Blake grinned back and touched the small of her back as she turned, guiding her to the only exit he could see. There was a large balcony, which was probably full of smokers, but the room was stifling and he didn't care.

"Excuse me." A loud voice boomed through the speakers, making him turn. "May I have your attention please?"

Blake groaned. Just as he'd been about to escape... "Want to make a run for it?" he murmured, leaning down to whisper into Saffron's ear. Her hair smelled like perfume, and it was soft against his cheek when she tipped her head back.

"I think we need to stay," she whispered in reply, dark brown eyes locked on his for a second. "As much as I'd love to disappear."

Blake shrugged. He would have happily disappeared and made a phone bid, but he wasn't about to leave the most interesting woman he'd seen all evening. Her dark red hair stood out in a sea of bright blondes and raven-haired heads, the color subtle but stunning. And in a room full of slim woman, she seemed even smaller, but not in a skinny way. Blake had noticed the way she was standing when he'd first seen her, her posture perfect, limbs long yet muscled, her body even more sculptured up close than it had appeared from afar. He was intrigued.

"Thank you all for being here tonight to raise funds for underprivileged children right here in New York City," the host said. Blake was tall, so even from the back of the room he could see what was going on, but he doubted Saffron would be able to see a thing. She was almost a head shorter than him. "Funds raised tonight will help to provide a winter assistance package for under-twelve-year-old children who don't have the basics to help them through our harsh colder months. They will receive a warm coat, shoes, hat, pajamas and other things so many of us take for granted."

Blake glanced down at Saffron. He watched her raise the slender glass to her mouth, taking a sip. He did the same, even though champagne wasn't his usual drink of choice.

"This is my friend's piece," Saffron said, meeting his gaze for a moment. "She's been working on this on and off all year, as part of her latest collection."

Blake pulled the brochure from his inside jacket pocket and stared at the first painting on the crumpled paper. He wasn't the type to get superexcited over art—all he cared about was making a sizable donation to a worthy cause—but he didn't dislike it. The bright swirls of multicolored paint looked interesting enough, and a quick scan over the bio told him the emerging artist could be one to watch. If he got a worthwhile, long-term investment for his donation, he'd be happy.

"We'll open the bidding at five hundred dollars," the auctioneer said, taking over from the host.

Blake raised his hand just high enough for the spotter to see. The bidding quickly moved up to five thousand dollars, and Blake stayed with it, nodding each time now that he was being watched. He didn't like drawing attention to himself, and from the look on Saffron's face when the bidding stopped at just over ten thousand, even she had no idea it was him pushing the price up. He was buying on behalf of the company, so to him it was small change, but he was certain it would be exciting for an emerging artist trying to make a name for herself.

"She'll be thrilled!" Saffron said, eyes bright as she connected with him. "All the other artists are so well-known, and..." She narrowed her gaze and he laughed.

"What?"

"Why are you smiling like that?" she asked.

Blake grinned. "I bought it," he said simply. "Hopefully she'll be superfamous one day, and I'll have a good story to tell and a decent investment on the wall of my office."

Saffron raised her glass and clinked it to his. "You're crazy."

"No, just in a generous mood." Blake had done his good deed, and now he was ready to go. The auctioneer started all over again, and he placed a hand to the small of Saffron's back. "Meet me outside? I just need to sign for the painting." He'd intended on buying two pieces, but he decided to make a donation with his purchase instead.

He watched as she nodded. "Sure."

Blake paused, hoping she wasn't about to walk out on him, then decided it was a risk he was just going to have to take.

"You never did tell me which café you work at."

She just smiled at him. "No, I don't believe I did."

When she didn't elaborate, Blake walked backward a few steps, not taking his eyes off her before finally moving away. He was used to women throwing themselves at him, wanting his money, being so obvious with their intentions. Saffron was different, and he liked it. There was no desperation in her eyes, no look as though she wanted to dig her claws in and catch him, and it only made him want to get to know her all the more. If she genuinely didn't know who he was right now, then he could be himself, and that was a role he hadn't been able to play in a very long time.

Saffron watched Blake from across the room. She'd been dreading coming out, not looking forward to making small talk and having people ask about her injury, but so far no one had really bothered her. Until Blake. She had no idea who he was or if she was supposed to know who he was, but he'd purchased Claire's painting as if it were no big deal, so he either had money or worked for a company that had told him to spend up. Either way she didn't care, but she was definitely curious.

The night air was cool when she moved out, but the large balcony was virtually empty. There was a couple kissing in the corner, obscured by the shadows, so Saffy walked closer to the edge, admiring the view. She'd never tire of New York. The vibrant atmosphere, the twinkling lights, the fact the city never seemed to sleep. It had a vibe about it that she'd never known anywhere else in the world, and for the first time in her life she felt as if she belonged, as though she was where she was supposed to be.

"Am I interrupting?"

The deep rumble of a voice behind her pulled her from her thoughts and made her turn. Blake was standing a few feet away, his champagne glass hanging from one hand and almost empty, his bow tie no longer perfectly placed against his shirt. The black satin tie was messed up, his top button undone and his jacket open. Saffy thought he looked sexy and so much more interesting than the rest of the suits she'd seen inside.

"Not at all. I was just admiring the city."

"You're not from here, are you?" he asked, moving closer and standing beside her, gazing down at the city as she glanced at him.

"Is my accent still that obvious?" Saffron frowned. She'd lived in New York for almost ten years now, since she was sixteen, and to her own ears she sounded more like a local than a girl from a small town in Kentucky.

"It's just a little twang every now and again. I can't quite put my finger on it, but..." Blake laughed. "Small town?"

Saffy gave him a stare she hoped looked evil before bursting out laughing. "A little place called Maysville, in Kentucky. But I haven't even been back in—" she sighed "—forever. You can take the girl out of the small town, but not the town out of the girl, right?"

Blake leaned against the railing and stared at her, his smile slow and steady as it spread across his face. She should have shrunk away from his stare, from his attention, but instead she bravely faced him. All the years she'd focused on her career, dancing from her childhood through her teens and then through almost all her twenties, she hadn't had time for boyfriends. But flirting with Blake felt good, and it wasn't as if she had anywhere else she needed to be or anything else she should be doing.

"So what's a girl from Maysville doing in New York?" he asked.

Saffy raised her glass and took a sip, wondering how much or little to tell him. "It's a long story."

His grin was infectious, the way it lit up his dark eyes and made a crease form at each side of his mouth. The man was gorgeous, textbook handsome with his dark hair and even darker features, his golden skin sexy against the white of his shirt.

"It just so happens," he said in his deep, raspy voice, "that I have all night."

"I'd rather hear about you," Saffy said, clearing her throat and trying not to become lost in his stare, hypnotized by his gold-flecked dark eyes.

"I'm guessing you want to open up about

yourself about as much as I like talking about *myself*," Blake said with a chuckle.

Saffron raised her glass again, realizing she was drinking way more than usual. She was usually too busy training to drink or socialize. Unless it had been with other dancers, she'd hardly seen anyone else, and she'd had to be so careful with her calorie count and her energy levels to waste on alcohol. She felt good tonight, though—alive and buzzing, even if it was due to the champagne and the smooth talker charming her.

"How about we agree to no personal questions then? I don't want to talk about work or my life," she admitted. She'd lived her work all her life as a ballerina, but every night she flexed her leg, only to be rewarded by ongoing shoots of pain, and she was reminded of what had happened. How little time she had left in the city she loved, and how quickly her dream had ended.

"It just so happens that I don't want to talk

about work, either," Blake said. "Want to go somewhere less..." His voice trailed off.

"Dull?" she suggested.

"Yeah, dull," he agreed, knocking back the rest of his champagne. "I hate these kinds of parties."

"I always thought it would be incredible to be asked to amazing parties, rubbing shoulders with the city's elite," Saffron admitted. "But I quickly realized that the part I liked was getting all dressed up. The parties weren't exactly as amazing as they looked from the outside once I'd attended a few."

"So you'd rather be somewhere more fun?" he asked with a chuckle.

"Ah, yes. I guess you could say that."

Saffron passed Blake her glass, not bothering to drink any more. She liked to stay in control, and if she was going somewhere with a man she hardly knew, she wasn't going to get drunk. Blake took it, turning his back for a moment as he found somewhere to leave them. She quickly pulled out her phone to text Claire.

Hey, you did great tonight. I'm heading out with the guy who bought your painting! If you haven't heard from me in the morning…

Saffy grinned as she hit Send. Claire would flip out, or maybe she'd just cheer her on. Her friend was always telling her to have more fun and stop taking life so seriously, but she wasn't the one in danger of having to pack her bags and go back to Maysville if she didn't get her job back. Saffron was serious because her job had demanded it, and she'd been happy to make it her life.

Her phone pinged back almost instantly.

Have fun. I'll track him down if I need to. xoxo

"Shall we go?"

Saffron put her phone back into her purse. "Sure thing."

Blake held out his arm and she slipped her

hand through, laughing to herself about how absurd the evening had turned out. She wasn't the girl who went on dates with strangers or disappeared with men and left her friends at a party. But nothing about the past month had gone according to plan, so she had nothing to lose.

"Do you like dancing?" Blake asked as they walked around the back of the crowd. He was leading her around the room, and she could feel eyes on them. Either because they were leaving too early or because of who he was. Or maybe she was just being overly sensitive and imagining it.

Dancing. When in her life hadn't she loved dancing? "Sometimes." If her leg didn't hurt like hell when she tried to dance, she'd love to.

"I was hoping you were going to say no."

Saffron laughed. This guy was hilarious. "It's a no. For tonight, anyway."

"Then why don't we go back to my place?" He must have seen the hesitation written all over her face, because he stopped walking and stared down at her. "Sorry, that came out all wrong."

"It's not that I don't want to…" Saffron actually didn't know what she thought, but she wasn't about to jump into bed with him. Maybe that's what he was used to? She hoped she hadn't read the situation wrong.

"I just meant that if we don't want to dance and we're bored here, it might be nice to just chill with a drink. Or we could find a nice quiet bar somewhere. It wasn't supposed to sound like that."

Saffy looked deep into his dark eyes, didn't see a flicker of anything that alarmed her. "Why should I trust you?" she asked.

He cleared his throat. "United States Army Officer Blake Goldsmith," Blake said, giving her a quick salute. "One of the only things I'm good at in life is keeping people safe, and that's about the only good reason I can give you."

She was more shocked that he was an officer

than the fact he'd asked her back to his place so fast. "You're in the army?"

"Was." Blake grimaced. "So much for not talking about my work life, huh? But yeah, you can trust me."

Saffron knew that just because he was a former officer didn't make him trustworthy on its own, but she wasn't actually worried about Blake. She felt as though she could take him at face value. What worried her was how he was making her feel, how desperate she suddenly was to know what it was like to meet a man and go home with him. Not that she could actually go through with a one-night stand, but the thought was making her tingle all over.

"So what do you say?" Blake asked. "I have a car waiting, so we can either jump in and head to my place or duck into a nearby bar."

Saffron passed a number over and collected her coat, snuggling into it before they stepped out into the chilly night air. On the balcony she'd been so busy admiring the view that she'd hardly noticed it, but now she was feeling the cold.

"Yours," she finally said. "It had better be warm, though."

Blake was holding a black scarf, and he tucked it around her neck, his hand falling to her back as they walked. "I promise."

She walked until he pointed out a black town car, and within seconds he was opening the door for her and ushering her inside.

"Tell me—how does a former soldier end up at a glitzy charity gala with a plush town car at his beck and call?" she asked, curious.

"Goldsmith Air," Blake said, pulling the door shut as he slid in beside her, his thigh hard to hers. "Family business, one I tried to steer clear of but somehow ended up right in the thick of."

Saffron knew what that felt like. "Sorry, I know we promised no work questions."

They only seemed to travel for a few blocks before they were outside a pretty brick building that looked old but had been renovated and kept immaculate. A huge glass frontage showed off a contemporary-looking café inside, the lights still on but the signs pulled in. She guessed he lived upstairs.

"So this is your local coffee place?" Saffron asked.

"I wake up to the smell of their coffee brewing, and by eight I've usually ordered my second cup for the day."

"They deliver to you?"

Blake gave her a guilty look before pushing the door open. "One of the perks of being landlord."

She didn't show her surprise. He was definitely not your average US Army veteran! Saffron stepped out and followed Blake as he signaled his driver to leave before taking her in through a locked security door that required him to punch a code in. They went in, and it locked behind them before he was punching in another code and ushering her into an elevator. Saffy admired the old-fashioned metal doors he pulled across, and within moments they were on the second floor.

"Wow." They stepped out into one of the hugest loft-style apartments Saffron had ever seen. Interior brickwork was paired with high-gloss timber floors, a stainless steel industrial-type kitchen taking center stage. She had to fight to stop her jaw from hitting the floor.

"So this is home?" she asked.

Blake shrugged. "For now."

He closed the door behind them and touched her shoulders, slipping her coat off and throwing it over the arm of a huge L-shaped sofa. Saffy spun around to ask him something and ended up almost against him. He must have moved forward, his arms instantly circling her, steadying her. She stared up at him, touched his arm, her fingers clasping over his tuxedo jacket as she became hypnotized by his stare.

Blake was handsome and strong and intriguing…all of the things that sparked her interest and made her want to run in the opposite direction but at the same time want to throw herself hard up against him.

"Are you okay?" he asked, the deep timbre of his voice sending a shiver down her spine.

Saffron nodded. "Uh-huh," she managed, still not pulling away, not letting go.

Blake watched her back, his eyes never leaving hers, and just when she thought she was going to step back, his face suddenly moved closer to her, *dangerously close*. Saffron's breath halted in her throat; her heart started to race. What was she even doing? In this man's apartment? In his arms? She barely even knew his name!

"Can I kiss you?" he murmured, his whisper barely audible, his mouth so near.

Saffy felt herself nodding even though she knew she shouldn't. But he clearly wasn't going to ask her twice. Blake's lips connected with hers, just a gentle, soft caress at first, his mouth warm to hers, unbearably gentle. She lifted her arms and tucked them around his neck as Blake deepened their kiss, his lips moving back and forth across hers as his hands skimmed down her back.

"I think we should get that drink," he muttered, barely pulling his lips from hers.

"Me, too," she whispered back. But her body had other ideas, pressed tight to him as he cupped her even tighter against him. Saffron had never been with a man she didn't know, her only experience from the one relationship she'd had with a dancer she'd performed alongside. But right now she wanted Blake, and no amount of willpower was going to let her move away.

Blake's groan was deep as he scooped her up, lifting her heels clean off the ground and walking her backward to the closest sofa. She only had a second to gaze up at him, a bare moment to wonder what the heck she was doing as he ripped off his tie and discarded it, staring down at her, his big body looming above.

And then he was covering her, his body over hers. Saffy lifted her mouth up to his, met his lips and hungrily kissed him back. She knew it was all types of wrong, but tonight she was going to be bad. If this was one of her last weekends in New York, then she was going to make the most of it. Her career might be over, but it didn't mean her life had to be.

CHAPTER TWO

SAFFRON OPENED HER eyes and quickly closed them. She groaned and pulled the covers over her head. She'd never had firsthand experience with what to do the morning after, and nothing clever was springing to mind. What had she been thinking?

"Morning."

She took a deep breath and slowly slipped the covers down, clutching them tight to her chest as she sat up. Blake was standing in the doorway, looking just as chiseled and sexy and gorgeous as he had the night before. No wonder she'd ended up in his bed. He crossed the room and sat on the bed beside her.

"Ah, morning," she finally stammered, clearing her throat and trying to pull herself together.

She didn't usually lack in confidence, but then again she didn't usually have to deal with handsome men so early in the morning. Saffron ran her tongue over her teeth, wishing she could have had ten minutes in the bathroom before having to face Blake.

"So I need to show you something," he said, eyebrows drawn together as he leaned closer.

It was only then she realized he was holding an iPad. Curious, she reached for it.

"What is it?"

"You know how we didn't want to talk about our personal lives or our work?"

Saffy nodded. She didn't understand what he was trying to tell her. Until she looked at the screen.

"Oh," she blurted.

"I think we probably *should* have had that conversation," Blake muttered. "Maybe we could have taken a back exit and made sure no one saw us."

Saffy kept hold of the covers with one hand

and swiped through the photos with the other. There was Blake with his hand to her back, Blake laughing, her laughing with her head tipped back and her eyes locked on his, and there was them getting into his town car. Paired with headlines screaming that Blake was one of the city's most eligible bachelors and naming her as one of ballet's finest forgotten stars. The description stung.

She swallowed away the emotion in her throat, the familiar burn behind her eyes that always hit when she thought about her career. When she passed the iPad back and glanced up at Blake, she wished she hadn't.

"Hey, it's not so bad," he said, discarding the iPad and leaning over. He reached for her hand and lifted it, kissing the soft skin on the inside of her arm.

Saffy smiled. *This* was how she'd ended up in his bed! He was so smooth yet seemed so genuine at the same time, although hearing that he was such a prized bachelor only made her wonder if he'd expertly played her to get her into bed.

"You're really upset about it, aren't you? I was hoping you wouldn't think it was that big a deal being papped."

She shrugged. "I don't care about being seen with you, or the photos. It's the headlines that sting," Saffy admitted.

Blake looked confused. "I'm not sure I'm following. You do realize that the whole bachelor thing has been completely blown out of proportion, right? It's rubbish."

Saffy shook her head. "It hurts to read that I'm a washed-up former ballerina. Sometimes the truth stings more than we realize."

Blake kept hold of her hand, staring into her eyes. "You look far too young to be washed up, surely."

"I'll give you points for being kind, but I'm not too young, not in the ballet world. My body broke down on me, so I'm out."

He chuckled. "By out, you mean injured,

right? Taking some time out? From what I've read this morning, you're pretty incredible."

Now it was Saffy chuckling. "You've been googling me?"

He shrugged. "Yeah. I'm an early riser. I saw this, and I've been reading up about you ever since."

She liked that he was at least honest. He could have lied and not admitted to it, but he was obviously curious about who he'd spent the night with. And if she was honest, she was starting to get pretty intrigued about him, too.

"What did it say?" Saffy wasn't clutching the sheet quite so tightly now, not as concerned as she had been about him seeing her.

"From what I've read, you came to New York as a teenager, wowed all the right people and eventually landed your dream role as lead in *Swan Lake* last year."

Saffron smiled. "Sounds about right." She wasn't sure she wanted to talk about it, not anymore. For years ballet had been her life, since she was a little girl in love with the idea of being a pretty dancer to a determined teenager and a dedicated adult. She'd lived and breathed her dream all her life, which was why she was at such a loss now. How did anyone move on if they'd lost the one thing that meant more to them than anything else?

Blake surprised her by stroking her face, his thumb caressing her cheek as he stared into her eyes. "I know the feeling."

She smiled, but it was forced. There was no way he knew how she was feeling. "You don't happen to have coffee, do you?" she asked, hoping he'd say *yes* then go and make her a cup so she had a little privacy.

"Sure do." Blake pulled back then rose, and the moment was over. He looked down at her, his height imposing. He was already dressed, barefoot but wearing dark jeans and a plain white tee.

Saffy waited for him to go then quickly scanned for her clothes. She hardly even remembered how they'd gotten to the bedroom. From what she could recall, her dress was in the living room wherever he'd thrown it, but her underwear was somewhere in the bedroom. She jumped up, taking the sheet with her. It wasn't until she had her underwear back on that she relaxed. Saffy looked around the room but he didn't have any clothes scattered, so she opened his closet and grabbed a sweatshirt. It was fleecy on the inside with a zipper, and given the size on her, she had to zip it all the way just to cover her body. Then she dashed into his bathroom, splashed some water on her face and ran her fingers through her hair to tame it. Given the fact she'd just woken and didn't have all her usual things with her, she didn't think she looked too terrible.

"So I—" Blake's deep voice cut off. "You look cute in my hoodie."

"Sorry." Saffron spun around, feeling guilty. "I should have asked first, but I didn't want to walk out half-naked."

Blake's laugh made her smile. He waved her toward him and turned, and she followed him out to the living area. He had music playing softly, just audible, and she tried not to gape at the apartment all over again. It was incredible, and it oozed money. He pointed to the coffee machine.

"I can make an okay black coffee, but if you want something fancy, I'll call downstairs."

Saffron shook her head. "I don't need fancy café coffee. Just give it to me however it comes, with a heaped teaspoon of sugar."

"Not what I expected from a ballerina. I thought all dancers would think of sugar as the devil and have eating disorders." Blake turned straight around then, his face full of apology. "Sorry, that was in bad taste. I didn't mean it."

She was used to it. "It's fine, and it's kind of true. There are plenty of dancers with problems."

"Yeah, still. Bad form. Want to tell me what happened?" he asked, pushing a big mug of steaming coffee across the counter and shoving his hands into his jean pockets as he stood watching her on the other side. "Sounds to me like you've had a rough year."

"Yeah, you could say that again," Saffy muttered.

"I have waffles and bacon on their way up, so you can tell me over breakfast."

She groaned. "Do I have to?"

His laugh made her smile. "Yeah, you kind of do."

Saffron hated talking about what had happened, didn't want to have to explain what she'd been through and what it meant for her, but breakfast did sound good and she wasn't about to run out. Especially not if there were paparazzi waiting outside to see if she'd spent the night.

"We could talk about what happened last night instead," he suggested, giving her a smile that made her want to slap him.

"Um, how about no?" she quipped straight back, heart racing.

"So let me guess," Blake started, walking away from her when a buzz rang out. She tracked him with her eyes, admired how tall and built he was. His hair was thick and dark, a full mop of it, and whereas last night it had been styled, this morning it was all mussed up. She liked him even better less groomed, although he had looked pretty hot in a suit the night before.

The next thing he was pressing a button. "Just give me a sec," Blake called over his shoulder before disappearing from the apartment.

Saffy let out a breath she hadn't even known she was holding. She reached for her coffee and took a slow, long sip. It was hot, but the burn felt nice down her throat, helped her to calm down somehow.

She could run. It wouldn't be her stupidest idea, and she could just grab her dress and bolt for it. Make up an excuse and dash past him. Get out of Dodge and never have to see him again or talk about what happened. She could even mail him back his hoodie, forget what she'd done. Only she wasn't sure she wanted to. The last few months, after the worst of her pain had passed, she'd been bored and miserable. She was working on autopilot, making coffee and serving people food, seeing her dreams disappear. It hadn't mattered what she'd done or how hard she'd tried, her leg hadn't healed fast enough, the ligaments badly torn, and with arthritis on top of it making the pain debilitating at best.

Blake had reminded her she was alive. If she hadn't met him, she'd have stayed another hour at the party, chatted with her friend, then gone home alone. Almost all her friends were dancers, and she wasn't in that world anymore.

So she stayed put, only leaving her seat on one of Blake's leather bar stools to retrieve her purse. It was tiny so she didn't have a lot in there, but she did have her foundation stick and some lip gloss, and she was keen to use both to make herself look half-decent. Plus she needed to text Claire.

She laughed. Her friend had already sent her three text messages, first wondering where she was, then asking how fab her night had been after seeing the article on some lame website. Then asking if she needed to send out a search party. Trust Claire to be scanning those types of pages as she ate her breakfast in the morning.

She sent her a quick message back.

I'm fine. He's gorgeous. Do you know anything about him?

The door clicked then, and she shoved her phone back in her purse. She hadn't had time to google him, and not being a native New Yorker, she didn't know the company name he'd mentioned the night before. He didn't strike her as a spoiled rich kid—more like a man who'd made his own money or his own way in the world, and she wanted to know more. Especially how he'd come to be listed as an eligible bachelor worthy of paparazzi.

"Breakfast is served," he announced.

Saffron stood and made her way back to the bar stool. "Mmm, smells delicious." Now she had clothes and some makeup on, she was a lot less self-conscious.

"Waffles with whipped caramel cream and fresh fruit. I went with sweet." His grin was naughty and she laughed at him.

"Can I just set the record straight about last night," she said, cringing at the way the words had come out.

"Sure. But you don't have to explain anything, if that's what you're worried about."

She sighed, taking the plate he held out to her. It did look delicious, the waffles thick and square, with pineapple and blueberries piled beside a swirl of the cream. "I just don't want you to think I do this sort of thing all the time."

He joined her around the other side of the counter, sitting down and passing her a knife and fork. "I kind of got that impression when you were peeking out at me from beneath the covers this morning with a horrified look on your face."

"Really?" She had to give it to him—he hadn't turned out to be a jerk the morning after.

Blake leaned over, smiling before dropping his mouth to hers, not giving her a second to hesitate. His lips were warm and tasted of coffee, his hand soft as he cupped the back of her head. He kissed the breath from her then pulled back, lips hovering as he stared down at her. Saffy felt the burn of heat as it spread up her neck, every inch of her body tingling from the unexpected kiss.

"You're too cute," he said with a grin, digging into breakfast like he hadn't just kissed her as if it was their last kiss on earth.

"And you're too suave for your own good," she muttered, stabbing her waffle with the fork, irate that he'd had such a visceral effect on her. "I'm guessing most of the women you bed are happy to drag you into bed the moment they lock eyes on you."

She had no idea why she was so mad with him when all he'd done was kiss her, but something about his attitude had gotten under her skin.

"Hey," he said, setting down his fork and turning to face her. "I meant it as a compliment, not to get you all fired up."

She went back to her breakfast, ignoring him.

"And I haven't exactly had the chance to meet a whole lot of ladies since I've been back. First I moved back home, then when I finally took over this place, I was spending more hours in the office than anywhere else. I haven't had time for socializing, other than when I've had to for work."

"You mentioned you were in the army," she said, calmed down and not so ready to jump down his throat. She'd seriously overreacted before.

"In another lifetime, yeah," he said, but he looked away as if he wasn't at all interested in talking about that other life. "Anyway, we're supposed to be talking about you. Tell me what happened. Why aren't you dancing now?"

Blake was intrigued. He'd bedded her already, and most of the time that was when his interest stopped, but she was something else. Even before he'd seen the blog post about them leaving the benefit together, which his sister had been so kind as to forward to him with a message that this one sounded a whole lot more promising than the airheads he'd been photographed with other times.

Blake kept eating his waffles, not wanting to stare at her and make her uncomfortable. He believed her that this wasn't her usual scene—she'd looked like a deer in headlights when he'd come back into the bedroom after hearing that she'd woken. His first instinct had been to dive straight back under the covers, until he'd seen her face and changed his mind. He still wanted her—he just wasn't going to be so forward.

Having a late breakfast with her and relaxing for once was making it clear he'd been way too focused on work the last few months. He'd become so determined not to buckle under the pressure and settle down, just because it would be good for business, but he was starting to realize he'd been missing out.

Saffron's red hair looked darker in the morning. Maybe it was the lack of bright lights, but it still looked incredible. The richest color against skin the lightest, barely there shade of gold, and dark brown eyes that just kept on drawing him in. He cleared his throat and set down his fork.

"Come on, what happened? Maybe I can help?" He doubted it, but he wanted to hear the story, and if she needed help finding work or someone to assist her with whatever injury she had, he did have helpful contacts.

His phone buzzed and he quickly glanced at it, not wanting to be rude by picking it up. He could read just enough of the text to see it was from his assistant and that the investor he'd been trying to impress had seen the paparazzi story. *Great.* Just when he'd been making some headway, now he was going to be labeled the rich playboy again.

"Nobody can help me," she said in a low voice. "Most dancers get injured and that's it, they're injured. Me, I'm out. Which means my career is over, because soon I'll have to go home with my tail between my legs, the washed-up former ballerina. I don't have enough money to stay here without working, and my physical therapy and specialist bills are crazy."

Blake frowned, forgetting the text and focusing on Saffron. "There's no other way for you to stay here?"

Saffron picked at her food, taking a mouthful that he was sure was a delaying tactic. When she finally looked up at him, her eyes were swimming. Big brown pools of hurt, bathed in unshed tears.

"I had a dream of dancing with the best ballet companies in the world, right from when I was a kid. I used to practice so hard, train my heart out and eventually it paid off." He listened as she blew out a big breath, sending a few tendrils of shorter hair around her face up into the air. "My hours of practicing got me noticed at the Lexington Ballet School in Kentucky, and eventually it turned into a dance scholarship with the New York Ballet Company. I started training there, danced my heart out and eventually went on to be an apprentice by the time I was eighteen."

"Wait, you moved to New York on your own *before* you were even eighteen? How old were you when you got the scholarship?" He knew plenty of models and other creative types started their careers early, but he'd never really thought about teenagers making such a big leap on their own. "Your parents didn't come, too?"

She shook her head. "Nope. Just me. I stayed with a relative for the first few months, then I moved into an apartment with some other dancers. I was only seventeen when I officially went out on my own, but I was so determined and focused on what I was doing that my parents didn't have any other choice. I would have resented them for the rest of my life if they hadn't let me come."

He got that. They'd let her follow her dream, and he admired any parent who encouraged their kids. "And then what? You make it sound like your career has already ended, like there isn't any hope." Blake hated hearing her talk as if it was over. She was doing what she wanted to be doing, and nobody was trying to hold her back, stifle her dreams.

"I tore three ligaments in my leg one night when I was dancing *Swan Lake*. I was finally in the role I wanted, as the lead, and I didn't even dance for an entire season at the top before my accident." She was looking away now, couldn't seem to meet his gaze. Blake wanted to reach for her, but he didn't, *couldn't*. The pain of what he'd lost and left behind was too raw for him, and he was barely coping with it on his own without having to help someone else.

"You could recover from that," he said gently, careful to choose the right words.

"No, I won't. I have a form of arthritis that I've battled for years. It first showed when I was stressed over a big performance, and in the past my doctors have been able to manage it. But from what I've been told, we're past that point now. That's why I'm out, why they wouldn't just let me stay on leave due to injury. They don't ever expect me to make a full recovery."

Blake steeled his jaw, hating that someone had had the nerve to put a damper on her dreams. On anyone's dreams. As far as he was concerned, the fight was worth it until the very last.

"You need to see more specialists, research more treatment, get your body strong again," he told her, wishing his voice didn't sound so raspy and harsh. "You can't take no for an answer when you're so close to living that dream."

Her eyes were angry, glaring when she met his gaze. "Don't you think I've done everything? As much as I could?"

He held up both his hands. "Sorry, I didn't mean to jump down your throat like that. I just..."

"I don't need to be told what to do," she said angrily, still holding his stare. "The only thing that will save me now is winning the lottery or a miracle. Money is the only way I can stay a part of this world, to keep searching for help, trying to keep training. Either money or a new treatment to help me get back on stage." She slumped forward, looked defeated. "Instead I'll be back in Hicksville, the girl who had so much potential and still ended up a nobody."

Blake bunched his fists, wished there was something he could do. He didn't know why her situation made him so angry, but it did.

Just then his phone buzzed and he glanced at it quickly. He read the screen, cursed his sister for wanting to be so involved in his love life.

So? Spill! Is she really a ballerina? She looked gorgeous. Keep this one!

Blake didn't bother replying, not about to engage with his younger sister over anything personal. And then he looked up and found Saffron watching him, her full lips parted, dark eyes trained on his.

She needed a way to stay in New York. He needed a wife.

He pushed his sister from his mind and pulled his bar stool closer to Saffron's, thinking that she was the most intriguing, beautiful woman he'd met in a long time. He didn't want to be married to anyone, but the truth was, he needed to be. That text just before was a slap-in-the-face kind of reminder. He was at the helm of a family business that was worth tens of millions of dollars, and he needed to maintain the right image. They were negotiating for a huge contract, one worth millions over the next two years alone, not to mention the investors he was trying to bring on board to grow the business.

But his biggest potential investor had made it beyond clear that he was worried about Blake's playboy status, didn't like the fact that he wasn't settled down and married. They were rich men with strong family values, the kind his own father had always managed to impress. Being married could be the key to finalizing those deals, and no matter how much he'd tried to pretend otherwise, it was true, which meant he had some serious damage control to do.

He reached for his coffee and drained it. Real marriage wasn't something he wanted, hadn't been on his agenda since the day his first love had walked away from him as though what they'd had meant nothing. He could still feel the cool sting of betrayal as if it was yesterday. But if he could package a marriage of convenience into something that could work for both him and Saffron? Now that was something he'd be willing to do.

CHAPTER THREE

BLAKE CONTINUED TO sip his coffee, watching Saffron. She was beautiful. She was talented and accomplished. She was interesting. If he had to pick a wife on paper, she was it.

"So come on, spill," she said, setting her knife and fork down, surprising him by the fact she'd actually finished her entire breakfast. "The more you tell me you don't want to talk about yourself, the more I want to know."

He shook his head. "No."

Saffron's laughter made him smile. "What do I have to do then? To make you tell me?"

Now it was Blake's laughter filling the space between them. "Marry me."

Her smile died faster than it had ignited, falling from her mouth. She stared back at him, eyebrows drawing slightly closer together. "I think I misheard you."

Blake smiled, knew he had to tell her his plan carefully, to sell the idea to her instead of having her run for the door and get a restraining order against him. She was probably thinking he was a nut job, some kind of stalker who was obsessed with her after one night together.

"Look," he said, spreading his hands wide as he watched her. "If you married someone like me, you would have access to the best medical treatments, and you could stay in New York without any worries."

She did a slow nod. "Funnily enough, I've been joking about that with my friends for weeks—that I need to find a wealthy husband. But I'm used to having a successful career and standing on my own two feet."

Blake shrugged. "What if we did it? If we got married so you could stay in New York and get back on your feet, so to speak? I could pay for any specialist treatment you need to get you dancing again."

Her gaze was uncertain, maybe even cool. He couldn't figure out exactly what she thought now that her smile had disappeared. "I know why it would be good for me, I just don't get why you'd want to do it. What's in it for you? Why would you want to help me?"

"Marriage to a beautiful ballerina?" he suggested.

"Blake, I'm serious. Why would you marry me unless there's something in it for you? A hidden catch?"

"Look, plenty of people marry for convenience. Gay men marry women all the time to hide their sexuality if they think it's going to help their career or please their family."

She sighed. "Well, I know you're not gay. Unless you put on the performance of your life last night, that is. And anyway, I know plenty of gay people, and it hasn't hurt their careers at all, to be honest."

"Well, you're a dancer. Corporate America isn't always so accepting, even if they pretend to be."

"Back to you," Saffron said, studying him intensely, her eyes roving over his face. "Tell me now, or I'm walking out that door."

Blake wasn't about to call her bluff. Just because she needed a boost in finances didn't mean she was automatically going to say yes to marrying a stranger.

"Running my father's company was never part of my plan," he told her. "Now I'm CEO of a company that I'm proud of, but not a natural fit for. It's not the role I want to be in, but there's also no way I'm about to let that company fall into the wrong hands. I need to keep growing it, and I'm working on two of the biggest deals in the company's history."

"I hear you, and I'm sorry you don't like what you do, but it doesn't explain why you need a wife. Why you need to marry *me*?"

Blake didn't want to tell her everything, didn't

like talking about his past and what he'd lost to anyone, why he didn't want a real wife, to open himself up to someone again. Eventually he'd have to tell her, otherwise she'd end up blindsided and their marriage would be uncovered as a sham, but not right now. Not until he knew he could trust her.

"I'm sick of the whole tabloid thing, the paps following me because some stupid magazine announced that I was one of New York's most eligible men." They'd called him the Billion Dollar Bachelor, the headlines had screamed out that women should be fighting over the former soldier back in the city as a corporate CEO and he hated it. Hated the attention and being known for his family's money after doing everything in his power to prove his own worth, make his own way in the world. But most of all he hated that people he most needed to impress right now read the rubbish being written, viewed him as a playboy, were unsettled by the fact that he *wasn't* settled.

"My dad built up the company as a family business, and our clients like that, especially a large-scale investor I've been working on for months. I don't want them to start thinking the company isn't going to continue to succeed because some loser rich-kid playboy is at the helm, and if I can set the right image now, it won't matter if I'm not married in a few years' time because the deals will be done."

Saffron didn't say anything when he paused, just stared at him.

Blake laughed. "Plus I'd like to get my mother and two sisters off my back. They're driving me crazy, trying to set me up all the time." He stood, pushing his hands into his pockets, watching, waiting for a reaction. He probably shouldn't have added the joke about getting them off his back. "So what do you think?"

"What do I think?" she muttered. "I think you're crazy!"

"We can talk through the details later, but please just think about it."

"Wow," Saffron said, holding up her hand. "I need time to think, to process how absurd this is."

"It's not that absurd," he disagreed.

"This is only-in-the-movies absurd," she fired back. "I'm not saying no, but I can't say yes right now, either."

Blake nodded. "I need to head in to the office. Why don't you stay here a bit, take your time and meet me back here tonight if you decide to say yes. I can get the paperwork and everything sorted out pretty quick, and we can go choose a ring together tomorrow."

Saffron shook her head, smiling then bursting into laughter. "I can't believe you're actually serious, that I'm not just being punked right now."

"Sweetheart, I'm deadly serious."

Blake took a few steps forward, touched her chin gently and tipped her face up, his thumb against her smooth skin. He slowly lowered his head and dropped his lips over hers, plucking softly at her lips.

"So we'd actually be married?" she asked, breathless, when she pulled back, mouth still parted as if she was waiting for more.

"Yes," he said, thinking how cute she looked in his hoodie. "You can set the boundaries, but we need it to look real."

He bent and kissed her again, softly.

Saffron could hardly breathe. She'd been outside for at least ten minutes, but her lungs still felt as though they couldn't pull in enough air. Marry him? How could he have asked her to marry him? They'd spent one night together—but marriage? Did she need rescuing that bad?

She pushed through a crowd of people passing on the street to reach a bench seat, dropping the second she found one. Could she actually marry a man she didn't even know, just to stay in New York? Just to get her career back on track, if that was even possible? She wished she could laugh it off and tell him there was no way she'd accept his proposal, but the truth was that it was the perfect solution for her. If it was the only way to give her recovery one last, real shot… Saffron gulped and turned her attention to the people walking past. Tried to lift her thoughts from Blake and failed.

What she needed was a piece of paper and her laptop. She would do what she always did— make a list of all the pros and cons, just like when she'd been offered the scholarship to dance with the New York Ballet in the first place. When she was sixteen, the list had been heavy on the pros and low on the cons, the only drawbacks coming from her parents, who wanted her to stay and didn't understand how desperately she wanted it. This time her list might be more balanced.

Marriage had always seemed so sacred to her, so special, but… She held her breath then slowly blew it out. Dancing was all she had. It was her life. If getting that back, having the one thing in the world back that meant so much to her, meant having to get married, then she had to consider it. Dancing had been her salvation. Could Blake really help her get that back?

Her phone buzzed and she picked it up, seeing it was Claire. She'd been out of touch with most of her dancing friends for the past couple of months, finding it too hard to hear about ballet and what they were training, the pain like a knife to her heart. But Claire had been there for her, been different and she'd enjoyed being part of her arty world.

"Hey," Saffy said when she answered.

"You're not still there, are you?" Claire giggled. "I still can't believe you did it. You're usually such a prude!"

Saffy laughed. "I am not a prude! Just because you have loose morals."

Now it was Claire in fits of laughter. "I'm not loose, I just don't see the point in saying no to a good time. Obviously my amazing personality has rubbed off on you."

Saffron felt better already after talking to Claire. "He..." Saffy changed her mind, not wanting to tell her. Claire was pretty open-minded, but even she might think it was crazy to consider the proposal.

"What? Tell me what you were going to say! He was amazing, wasn't he? Tell me more!" her friend begged.

Saffy sighed, the weight of her decision hanging heavy. "He was amazing, incredible, but..." Her voice trailed off again. "He wants to meet again tonight."

"Awesome! He's seriously hot stuff. Not to mention he paid up big-time for my painting. I've already had phone calls from buyers asking about my commissions and existing work."

If there hadn't been the whole marriage thing to consider, she would have been more excited. Giddy over being with a man like Blake, a man who'd made her pulse race and her mind forget all about what she'd lost while she'd been with him. She'd have liked the idea of getting to know him better, *dating* him, not marrying him.

"Good, you deserve it. And he was lovely. I'm just not sure about everything."

Silence stretched out between them, just long enough for it to be noticeable. "You're thinking about having to go back home?"

"Yeah." Saffy wasn't lying; she just wasn't telling her everything. Besides, Claire would be the one person to know the truth if it did happen, that she'd only met Blake the night before. She trusted her not to say anything, to keep her secret, but she just wasn't ready to open up about it yet, not when she was still trying to process it herself.

"Do you have any more doctors to see? Any other specialists you could visit or anything?" Claire asked. "Can you afford to keep going for a bit longer?"

Saffy shook her head, even though she knew Claire couldn't see her. This was why she was considering the marriage—this was why she *had* to. "No," she murmured. "I've done everything. There's no one left to see, or at least no one I can afford now, and I'm like damaged goods on the dance scene. If I dance again, there's only one company I want to be with, and that's a firm no right now."

"Fight till the bitter end, Saffy. Don't go quitting until you have no other options left."

Saffron had no intention of giving up until the last; it had been her attitude all her life. But even she had to admit that when it was over, it was over.

"There's one last thing I have to consider," she told Claire. "One last option."

"Give it a go—you owe it to yourself."

"I'm going to go, I have a few jobs to get done," Saffy said, wanting to end the call so she could think some more. She started to walk, the familiar twinge in her knee bearable at a walk when she was wearing heels. Barefoot it was almost unnoticeable. It was when she tried to push herself harder or dance that it really hurt. "Enjoy the weekend."

"You, too. Give me a call tomorrow so I can hear all the juicy details from tonight."

Saffy said goodbye and kept walking, suddenly realizing how terrible she must look. She was wearing her blue satin dress, her hair was tangled, and her heels weren't exactly daytime wear. Thank goodness there had been no cameras flashing when she'd exited out the back of Blake's building, through the café. Her career being over was bad enough—the last thing she needed was for the public to see pictures of her looking like she was right now.

Marriage. No matter how hard she tried to clear her head, Blake's proposal was the only thing on her mind. And she was pretty certain that, like it or not, she was going to have to say yes.

Blake sat in his office, staring out the huge windows that bordered two sides. It was a stunning corner office—luxurious and extravagant—but it didn't feel like his. For two decades it had been his father's office, and he'd been in it numerous times, often when his father was trying to convince him that the company was where he should be. That it should be his dream, as if he should grow up to be a carbon copy of the man who'd raised him. But Blake had never wanted to be his father, had had dreams of his own, dreams that were still with him that he'd been forced to leave behind.

He stood and walked to the window, restless being inside and having to stare at paperwork and sign contracts. The city was alive below him, people milling everywhere, and he wished he could just disappear in the crowd and leave his responsibilities behind. But he'd made the decision to come back, and he wasn't a quitter.

"This is your life, son. You're my eldest, and I expect you to take over the business. To look after your family."

The words had echoed in his mind long before

his father had died, but now they were never ending. Every time he wanted to walk away, they haunted him, kept him awake at night. He was the eldest, and he'd always had a sense of responsibility that his younger brother and sisters had never had. But it hadn't stopped his brother from wanting to run the company, to absorb everything their father had to share and teach.

Everything had been going to plan—Blake was doing what he loved, and his brother was shadowing their dad, learning the ropes, prepared to take over the company one day. Until everything had gone horribly wrong.

Blake clenched his teeth together and crossed the room, reaching for the whiskey his father had always kept in the office, filling one of the crystal tumblers he'd seen his father drink from so many times. He poured a small amount into the glass and downed it, liking the burn. *Needing* the burn.

The chill he'd felt when they'd died, when his mother had phoned him and he'd heard the choke in her voice, knowing the helicopter had gone down. He'd gotten there as fast as he could, been with the rescue team on the ground, seen the wreckage with his own eyes. At that moment, he'd known he had no other choice—he had to step up and take over the business just like his father had always wanted him to do. He'd lost so many good people in his life, but losing his father had never been something he'd thought about until it had happened.

Blake set the glass down again and went back to his desk. There were things he couldn't change, memories that would be with him forever, but the only thing that mattered right now was doing the best, given what life had served him. And Saffron would go a long way to helping make his life easier, making sure he secured the deals and the financial backing he needed to take the company to the next level. He needed a wife at his side, and she was the perfect match to him, could be the perfect, capable woman at his side…because they could enter into the relationship with a contract that gave them both exactly what they wanted.

He checked his phone. He'd half expected her to text or phone him after thinking about it, but then he'd also seen the determined look in her eyes, known that she was a fighter from the moment he'd heard about how she'd risen to the top. A ballerina who'd defied all odds and risen through the ranks to become one of New York's most respected dancers. It wasn't an easy path, and he doubted she would like having to do something she didn't want to do.

It was easy for him because it was a win-win situation. He would have a wife, a beautiful woman by his side who intrigued him, and they'd be divorced within the year. He didn't want a family, didn't want children, and he certainly didn't want an *actual* wife. They were things he'd dreamed of a decade ago, before the only person in his life he'd ever completely opened up to and been himself with had ripped out his heart and torn it to shreds. He wasn't ever going to put himself in that position again, just like he would never deceive a woman into marrying him without clearly setting out his terms.

Blake smiled and sat back down in the plush leather chair. Usually Saturdays were his favorite day to work, when the office was quiet and no one was around to bother him. But today his mind was wandering, and it was a stunning redhead on his mind that he couldn't stop thinking about. Whoever said he couldn't mix a little pleasure with business?

Saffron stared at the list she'd made, chewing on the end of her pen. It was a pretty short list. She leaned back into the sofa. There was no other way. Blake had just given her the perfect way to stay in the city, but being at the beck and call of a man like him was…scary. She shut her eyes, smiled when she thought about the night they'd shared.

She was going to do it. Saffy laughed out loud, feeling kind of crazy. Maybe she'd drunk too much the night before and it was still in her system, or maybe she was actually crazy, but she had to do it. She stood and flexed, grimaced when she tried to push up onto her toes and flex her muscles. The pain was tolerable, barely there compared to the excruciating pain she'd experienced at the time, but it still told her that things weren't right. That without some kind of miracle, she wouldn't be dancing anytime soon. But it didn't mean she couldn't keep her body strong and exercise.

She pulled on her trainers and laced them up, carefully stretching out her muscles just like her physical therapist had showed her. Her body was everything to her, and she had always taken care to stretch and warm up slowly, but now she had to treat it with even more care than ever before. Saffron rose up onto her toes, watched herself in the full-length mirror she had propped against a door. She held her arms out, tucked one leg up, bit down hard on her bottom lip as she flexed, forced herself to take the weight on first her good leg and then her bad.

No more. She released her lip from her teeth, expecting to taste blood she'd been biting so hard. The pain was there, was just as bad, and that meant she had to stop even though she would have loved to have tried to push through it.

Instead she grabbed her iPhone and stuck her earbuds in, planning on walking for an hour. She'd rather be running or dancing, but right now it was either walking and swimming or nothing at all. If she pushed herself too hard before she was ready, she wouldn't have the chance to make the same mistake again.

She checked the time before pulling the door shut behind her. She could walk for an hour or so, grab a coffee, then shower and head to

Blake's house. Money was tight, which was another pro on her list, because if she married him then she'd be living with him. If she didn't, it would look like the sham it was, and she knew he wanted to keep it real. Besides, he'd told her as much—that she wouldn't have to worry about finances.

Right away she could cut almost all of her expenses, and her back account was already screaming out in the red after the cash she'd spent on all sorts of alternative therapies in conjunction with the specialist's advice.

Saffron Goldsmith. It sure had a ring to it. She glanced at her finger. Tomorrow there could be a diamond sparkling there, a real ring, a ring that would tell everyone that she was engaged. She hadn't exactly been the type to dream of a wedding when she was a girl—she'd been too focused on her career—but it still seemed weird.

She breathed in the fresh air once she was outside and started walking, slow at first. In a few hours' time she was going to be saying yes to a man she hardly knew, which meant this could very well be her last little glimpse of freedom before she had another human being to answer to.

CHAPTER FOUR

SAFFRON SHUFFLED HER bag from hand to hand, hating that her palms were so sweaty. She usually got nervous only before a performance, and even then it always passed as soon as she stepped on stage. This was a weird kind of nervousness that she hadn't felt before.

She took a big breath and squared her shoulders before pushing the button to Blake's apartment. He didn't say anything through the intercom, but the door clicked and she opened it and let herself in, going up in the elevator. When the metal doors opened, she found him leaning on the doorjamb, eyes searching hers out.

"I see you've brought a bag," he said, not taking his eyes from hers.

She kept her chin up, didn't want to appear weak. She felt like a prey animal having to stand up to a predator, standing her ground and being brave even when all she really wanted to do was cower.

"I have," she said back.

"Well, then, come on in. *Fiancée.*"

Saffy gulped and stepped forward, walking straight past Blake and into the apartment. The apartment she lived in was like a shoe box in comparison, small enough to fit inside his five times over. The sprawling spaces reminded her more of places back home, where space wasn't at a premium.

"We need to establish some ground rules," she said, deciding to start how she wanted things to be, not wanting him to think he could boss her around.

"I'm all ears." His smile made him even more handsome, eyes twinkling as he watched her.

She wasn't going to let him rattle her with his gorgeous face. Or his gorgeous body. Although the way his arms were folded across his chest as he stared at her made his shirt strain across his biceps. Even worse was how chilled out he seemed about the whole thing.

"I want everything in writing," she began, setting down her bag and taking a seat on the same bar stool she'd been perched on earlier in the day. "I need to give up the lease on my place and know that I can live here while we're married, for at least a year. I'll continue to pay for my own personal things, but you need to cover all my medical expenses, including any new specialists I find. I'm doing this only because I think there's a chance I could find someone to help me if I have the funds."

He raised an eyebrow, one side of his mouth kicked up at the sides. "Is that all? Or do you have a full list of ransom details?"

Saffy cracked a smile. "That's it."

He walked toward her, and a shiver ran down her spine. She had the distinct feeling that he was the one in charge, even though he'd just agreed to her terms.

"I agree," he said simply. "In fact, I already have a contract for you to sign."

She laughed. "Your lawyer did up an agreement for you on a Saturday?"

His shrug told her this wasn't out of the ordinary. "We have him on a pretty good retainer."

"So just like that, you agree?" she asked. Once again, it seemed too good to be true. For her, anyway. "To funding me and promising that this will go on for at least a year?"

"Sure. I'll even let you keep the diamond ring as a separation gift when we part ways." He didn't look worried about anything. "I need this *marriage* to exist for at least a year, too, to make sure my investors sign on the dotted line and to ensure it doesn't look like a sham. Once I have everything in place, it won't matter whether I'm married or not."

His smile was wolfish now, and she wasn't

sure if he was joking or not. "You actually mean it about the diamond?"

"Yes. We can pick something tomorrow." She watched as he picked up a thick envelope from the coffee table. "This is some light reading for you—sign when you're ready."

She nodded. "Okay."

"I'm going to leave you to read it, give you a bit of space. Maybe a couple of hours for you to look over the paper, sign, and take a walk around the apartment without me being here. Feel free to consult with your own attorney if you want to, but you'll find that there's nothing in there not spelled out in plain English."

"Sure." It all seemed so weird, so formal, but she'd made up her mind and she was going to do it. There was no backing out now, not unless he had something sneaky in the contract that took her by surprise.

"We'll head out to dinner to celebrate," he said, passing her the envelope and reaching for her face, touching a stray tendril of hair and then running his thumb down her cheek.

She stared into his dark eyes, wishing she knew more about the mysterious man she was about to marry.

"My mother is going to love you," he said with a chuckle before stepping backward.

If only he loved her. She quickly pushed the thought away, checked herself. Blake was virtually a stranger—the last thing he'd feel was love for her! Maybe she was suffering from some sort of Cinderella complex, because it felt as if Blake was saving her, had ridden to her rescue and was offering her everything.

The everything part was true, but he was no Prince Charming. She was kidding herself if she saw him as anything other than a man who needed something and was prepared to do whatever he had to in order to make that happen.

"Your mother'd better love me," she finally managed in reply.

"Did I mention I also have two interfering sisters?" he asked as he shrugged into a jacket.

Saffy groaned. "Don't say anything else, or you might find the envelope unopened and me long gone." If only she had the power to do that, wasn't trapped in a corner with no other options. She'd still be interested in getting to know him better, but she sure wouldn't be jumping headfirst into marriage.

Blake just grinned and held up a hand. "See you soon. Anything you don't eat?"

She shook her head. "Not really."

"Good, I'll make us a reservation for seven. See you later on."

She watched him go, sat silently, until he had his hand on the door.

"Wait!" she called.

Blake turned, eyebrows raised in question.

"Why don't you stay? Then we can just talk through the whole thing." She didn't actually want to be left alone, didn't want to sit in silence trying to figure out legal jargon on her own.

Blake's smile made her heart skip a beat. "I thought you'd never ask." He shrugged off his jacket as fast as he'd put it on only moments earlier, dropping down onto the sofa, eyes still on hers. "You read, I'll answer questions."

She slowly ripped the envelope open, scanned a little of the first page before leaning on the bar and looking at Blake.

"So obviously there's a prenup," she said.

"Yep," he said. "Standard terms, including that if there were any children born during our marriage the child would be cared for." He laughed. "Obviously that's not in either of our plans, though, right?"

Saffy laughed straight back. "Have you ever seen a pregnant ballerina?" She definitely wouldn't be getting a penny from Blake, because there was no way she was getting pregnant, no way she *could* get pregnant.

"Which leads to the next clause, to ensure that every precaution is made to ensure no children *can* be conceived, something about blah-blah it not being part of either of our plans."

"Phew. Glad we got that sorted out," she said with a giggle, liking that she made Blake laugh again. His smile lit up his face, and it made her feel more relaxed. "Please tell me you have it in writing that I get to keep whatever rock you put on my finger?"

"Why, yes. The bride may keep the ring after separation or divorce. It'll be all yours once you've done your duty."

"Uh-huh," she said, scanning through a few more pages, seeing that everything he was saying was listed. And then she reached the part about the marriage being real, blushed as she looked up to find Blake watching her.

"We must live as a real husband and wife," she forced herself to say out loud.

"You're so cute when your face goes all pink," he said, rising and crossing the room.

She looked down, hating that she was so reactive when it came to him.

"It only stipulates that we have to live together at all times…that we remain faithful and don't speak to the media." He brushed past her, moving into the kitchen. "Beyond that, it's up to you. I just don't want anyone, from colleagues to housekeepers, not to believe that our marriage is real."

"So there's nothing in here you're trying to hide from me? Everything's as you say?" she asked, scanning though the pages again, pleased it wasn't a long document.

"I'm not trying to deceive you. It goes on to say that all your medical costs, including elective consultations and treatments, are covered. You have my word."

Saffy knew she needed to just sign it, that it was the best thing for her right now. So long as she didn't let herself get emotionally involved. She signed at the end, taking a pen from the kitchen counter that she could reach. Then there was a single document, just one page that fluttered out from beneath. From what she could see it was a separate contract.

This one was stamped confidential. She scanned it, realizing that this was the divorce contract. It was crazy—on the one hand she was signing a prenup, and on the other she was confirming a divorce was to take place when they both agreed it should, but in no longer than three years. She was to file for divorce, stating irreconcilable differences. Saffron hesitated, thinking of how long her own parents had been happily married, but she quickly pushed those thoughts away. This wasn't a real marriage. It was a convenient relationship for both of them, and they were both adults. There were no children involved, which meant that the only people that could be harmed by what they were doing were the two of them. The only thing she would have to be embarrassed about would be lying to her parents, because it wasn't exactly something she could keep from them. She'd never deceived them before about anything, had never lied to anyone she cared for, but this was her one chance to dance again and when it was all over she'd tell them the truth.

Saffy signed the second document, looking up and realizing how silent Blake had been.

"All done."

He exhaled loudly. "Guess it's my turn then." He leaned over her, his musky cologne making her wish she'd held her breath instead of inhaling. And then it was done.

"Take a look around. I'll make us a drink," he said with a wink.

"Mind if I take a shower?" She was dying to stand under hot water, needing some time to think.

"It's your home now. You can do whatever you like."

Saffron gulped and left him in the kitchen, going first into Blake's bedroom, taking a look around the very masculine space. The bed was made—a dove-gray cover paired with white pillows and a smattering of gray cushions against a black leather headboard. She'd already looked in his closet that morning and seen the bathroom, so instead of looking around more, she decided to just jump in the shower. Wash her hair and luxuriate in a bathroom that was bigger than her former bedroom, the floor-to-ceiling tiles reminding her of some of the lovely hotels she'd been fortunate to stay in when she'd been touring a few times. She went back out and got her suitcase, pleased to see that Blake was on the phone so she could just slip straight past him, putting her luggage in the middle of the bedroom.

Saffron stripped down, leaving her clothes in a puddle on the bathroom floor and turning the faucet on. The water was warm almost instantly, but she quickly walked out, naked, to retrieve her cosmetic bag that had her shampoo and conditioner in it. The shower was so good, the nozzle spraying so much water out and the steam feeling so good around her that she didn't want to get out. Instead she just shut her eyes and stood there, wishing she could stay there all day. Her hair was washed, the citrusy smell of her shampoo wafted around her, and all she had to do now was soap up her body…

"You need anything?"

Her eyes popped open and water blurred her gaze. Saffy quickly soaped herself and rinsed. Had he just walked in?

"Saffy? Do you still want that drink?" Blake's deep voice sent shivers down her spine, made her self-conscious with no clothes on.

"Just a sec!" she called back, hoping he'd stay in the bedroom and not actually walk on in.

Saffy turned the faucet off and jumped out, hurriedly reaching for a towel and rubbing it down her body then back up again. She was just about to dry her hair when his voice sounded out a whole lot closer.

"Hey. I wasn't sure if you'd heard me."

She wrapped the towel around herself and flung her hair back. Blake was standing in the doorway, looking straight in at her in the bathroom. Granted, she hadn't closed the door properly, but she hadn't expected him to walk in on her!

"Um, I just…" She stammered, knowing it was stupid being so body conscious, given the fact he'd seen her stripped bare less than twenty-four hours earlier, but she couldn't help it.

"Sorry, I didn't think you'd…" Blake was talking to her, but his eyes weren't on hers. They kept drifting down, and she held the towel a little tighter. "I can see this wasn't a good idea. I'll make you that drink."

"Uh, yeah, sure."

Blake was still watching her, but his eyes were trained on her face now. "This is weird, huh?"

She tucked the towel in at her breasts. "Um, yeah. Very weird."

Blake backed up. "I'll give you a minute to get, ah, dressed."

Saffy slipped to the floor in a puddle when he disappeared, her back against the glass of the shower. This was ridiculous! She was craving him, wanted him against her so she could kiss him all night, but at the same time she was a bundle of nerves about him even seeing her bare skin.

Maybe it was just because there was so much at stake now. Or maybe she just didn't want to admit that after being bored for so long after she'd had to quit dancing, she was finally feeling alive again and it scared her.

She picked herself up, dashed into the bedroom to get some clean underwear, and slipped on a big thick white terry cloth robe that she'd seen earlier in Blake's closet. She tied it around herself, liking how snuggly it was. It also covered up her body, which she thought might be a good idea in case Blake came back in. Saffy towel dried her hair, deciding to put on her makeup first and rub some moisturizer into her legs since she wanted to wear a dress out for dinner.

They weren't even married yet, and already she felt as if she'd lost control.

* * *

Blake sat on the sofa then jumped up and paced back toward the kitchen. He wasn't used to being so...rattled. Seeing Saffron in his bathroom, knowing exactly what was under the towel she'd had clasped to her slick wet body... He groaned. Maybe the marriage contract had been a bad idea. *A very bad idea.* She was supposed to make his life easier, and instead she was stopping him from thinking about anything else.

He glanced at the paperwork on the counter and then looked back toward his bedroom. It was all signed, which meant all that was left was for him to actually go down on bended knee for real so they had a story to tell everyone about their engagement.

Blake opened a bottle of wine, needing to take his mind off Saffron. There was something easy about what they'd agreed to, but for a man who'd sworn off marriage and family years ago, it was unsettling, too. He'd lived alone all his life unless he'd been working, when he'd been bunked down with his unit, and until Saffy he hadn't even brought a woman back to his apartment. And now he'd gone and broken all his rules, let someone get close to him, even though this time around he was in control of the situation. He was never going to be made a fool of again, never wanted to voluntarily feel hurt like he'd felt in the past, but so long as they both stuck to the rules…

"Dollar for them?"

Blake looked up, pulled from his thoughts. She was standing forlorn in the middle of the room, staring at him. Her hair was still damp, hanging loose and tumbling down over her shoulders, and she was wrapped in his robe. A robe he hardly ever wore, but his nonetheless. It was the second time he'd seen her in his clothes, and he was starting to more than like it.

"Nothing," he said, turning his body to face her. "Nothing important, anyway."

He watched as she shifted, looked uncomfortable. Blake had a feeling he wasn't going to like what she had to say.

"Is everything okay?"

She sighed loud enough for him to hear. "I don't know about you, but this whole thing just seems…"

"Unusual?" he suggested.

"Kind of uncomfortable," she said. "I don't know, I just don't know how to act around you. Last night I was me, or at least a version of me. But now…"

Saffron didn't seem to be able to finish her sentences, as though she was overly nervous. He stood but decided not to walk over to her, to keep some space between them instead of pushing her. The last thing he wanted to do was scare her off now.

"How about you finish getting ready for dinner," Blake said gently, trying his hardest to say the right thing. He had two sisters, so being around women and knowing what to say should be second nature to him, only for some reason it wasn't helping him right now. "Maybe we can take a step back, forget about the contract for a bit. We can pretend this is real if we like. Just actually date and try to ignore the marriage part to make it easier."

He had to fight a grin when her saw her lips kick up into a small smile.

"You really think we can go back? Trick ourselves that this is real?"

Not for a minute, because the only way he would ever propose to a woman was in a situation like this. "Sure we can," he said, trying to sound optimistic. "And if we can't do that, then there's no reason we can't be friends, enjoy the next year or so together." He knew that was a lie, too. Because there were plenty of ways they could enjoy being together, but strictly as friends wasn't what he had in mind right now or probably ever would with her.

Saffron turned and disappeared back into the bedroom, and within minutes he heard her hair dryer going. The beautiful ballerina would no doubt emerge a knockout, just like she'd looked last night.

He could be plenty of things to Saffron without having to open up, though. He had no interest in baring his soul to another human being, or reliving any of his past and opening up about anything. If he was in a real relationship, those things would be nonnegotiable, but with Saffron he could choose how much to divulge, how much of his true self to give. Because no matter what they pretended to the contrary, what they had was a contract. He'd fallen in love before, had his heart broken by someone he'd trusted more than anyone else. Fool him once, but never twice…

Blake took a sip of his wine and stared at the documents sitting in front of him.

It was done. He was officially about to become a married man.

Blake pulled his phone from his pocket and dialed his mother. He wanted to get it over and done with now, and he only had to phone one of the women in his family, because news spread like wildfire between his mom and sisters.

"Hello, darling."

"Mom," he said, clearing his throat. He could still hear Saffron's hair dryer, so he launched into what he had to say. "I know you've seen the pictures from this morning."

"Of course I've seen them. I'm just disappointed you've kept such an interesting woman hidden away from us."

If Saffron was really his fiancée-to-be, he would definitely be keeping her hidden from his family! "Mom, I should have told you, but we've just been lying low, getting to know each other without…"

"You don't have to explain yourself, sweetheart. I'm just happy that you're seeing such a fantastic young woman!"

"The girls have been googling her and showing you the results, haven't they." Blake had no doubt that they'd be all over the internet. There was no way his mother was that tuned in on her own; he'd bet they'd all been gossiping and flicking through web pages together.

"Of course!"

"Mom, I hope you're sitting down, because I have news."

"Blake! What is it?"

"I've asked Saffron to marry me."

"Girls!" His mother's screech forced him to pull the phone from his ear.

"I have to go, Mom. We're going out to dinner to celebrate, and I wanted to share the good news with you before anyone else found out."

"Could we join you? Meet this woman who's going to be my daughter-in-law?"

Blake could hear the excitement in his mother's voice, felt a pang of guilt for deceiving her. His mother got on his nerves at the best of times when it came to his personal life, and his sisters drove him crazy sometimes, but he loved them as fiercely as was humanly possible and lying to them made him feel worse than he'd expected.

"Let me take Saffron out tonight, just the

two of us. I promised her something special to celebrate," Blake said. "But we'll see you soon, okay? I won't keep her hidden away forever."

He wondered if his mother would even take the bait, if she'd be instantly suspicious, but then she was used to him keeping his personal life private. And as far as he knew, she'd been shielded from what his dad had done, had never been exposed to the truth of the only serious relationship he'd ever had before. Never known how much pain her eldest son had been in.

When he finally got her off the phone and managed to end the call, he glanced up to see that Saffron was sitting on the sofa. He'd been so engrossed in talking with his mom, staring out the window as day became night, that he hadn't even heard the hair dryer switch off.

"You heard all that?" he asked.

Saffron shrugged, still flipping through a magazine. "Mmm, some of it." She looked up. "Do you feel kind of guilty?"

He nodded. "Yes, but it's for the best."

"I'm going to have to put on the performance of my life for your mother, aren't I?"

Blake didn't want to scare her. "Look, she'll be so excited to meet you that she'll probably do all the talking. The real performance will be when I have you by my side at business functions. That's why I'm marrying you."

She didn't look worried about it.

Blake unbuttoned his shirt and stretched out. "Give me a minute to take a shower."

He could feel her eyes on him as he walked, knew she was watching him. His problem was that he didn't know how to behave, how to act. He wanted to forget everything and just… He steeled his jaw. Sex should be the last thing on his mind. He wasn't doing this for sex—he could get that without being married—but looking at Saffron made him think of one thing and one thing only.

He left her on the sofa and stripped, showering then tucking his towel around his waist when he was finished. He went back into the bedroom adjoining the bath and pulled out a fresh shirt. He dressed quickly, ran his fingers through his hair and put some product in.

When he went back out, Saffron was still sitting on the sofa where he'd left her.

"Ready?" he asked, voice sounding gruff to his own ears.

She stood. "Yep, ready."

He walked ahead, opened the door and stood back for her to follow. Her dress was short, cute and covered in sequins. It showed off her toned, slim legs, and there was plenty of skin for him to admire up top, too. Her top was loose but with a low front, hair flowing down her back. It was the hair that got him more than the skin, though. Because when he'd first woken after their night together, it had been her hair touching his skin, falling over his chest. Her hair that he'd stroked.

"Where are we going?" she asked.

Blake cleared his throat. He was lucky she

wasn't a mind reader. "Somewhere close. We can walk."

She shrugged her leather jacket on and they walked side by side, lights twinkling and showing the way along the road.

"I booked us in for Japanese. I'm thinking sushi, sashimi and teppanyaki."

Her smile was so innocent he wanted to reach for her and tug her closer. Maybe that was why he'd been drawn to her in the first place, not just because she was beautiful, but because there was something vulnerable about her. Something so unlike most of the women he met, a fragility that was tempered by how successful she'd been in her career.

"Are we sitting at the teppan table?" Saffron asked, her grin infectious. She was more excited child than grown seductress for a moment.

"We sure are. I thought you might like watching the food cooked in front of us."

She laughed. "You mean you thought it would

be a good distraction when we ran out of things to talk about."

Blake held up his hands. "Guilty."

They walked in silence a bit longer.

"This is the weirdest one-night stand I've ever had," Blake confessed. "It's kind of awkward, in a we-wouldn't-usually-see-each-other-again kind of way. It's like extending the morning-after part."

Her laughter was gone but her eyes were still twinkling with humor. "I wasn't lying when I said I hadn't had a one-night stand before. So the whole awkward-morning-after thing is all new to me."

"Well, let me tell you it's normally over really fast and then you forget about it." He chuckled. "Although if I'm honest, you might have taken a little longer to forget about."

"So no serious girlfriends? No ex-wives I should know about?"

The last thing Blake wanted to do was talk about his ex. With anyone. "Let's just say that my mother never thought I'd settle down. I've always made that pretty clear."

"Right," she said as he guided her into a restaurant. It was only a few blocks away, so the walk had been brief. "So you've preferred to be the party bachelor boy all your life?"

He kept his anger in check. The last thing he wanted was for her to think the same way about him that everyone else seemed to in this city. "I was too busy with my career to be the party boy, even though everyone seems to forget how long I was away serving."

Saffron seemed confused when she looked up at him. "I'm getting the feeling that there's someone who broke your heart. Someone you really don't want to talk about."

"So let's not talk about it," Blake ground out. It wasn't as if he had a problem talking about the dates he'd had or the women he'd been with—it was just one particular woman who still made him want to slam his fist into a wall. It wasn't because he still had feelings for her; it was the way she'd hurt him, the way his father had been able to hurt him so easily through her. "I'm starving. You?"

He listened to Saffron sigh, knew the sound and that it meant the conversation wasn't over. His sisters made the same noise all the time. But to her credit she didn't bring it up again.

Saffron stayed silent as they were taken to their table, sitting down and starting to toy with the menu. Blake couldn't stand it.

"Look, I didn't mean to shut you down like that, but there are just some things I don't want to talk about."

"Me, too, but we kind of need to know everything about each other."

"What do you want me to say?" he muttered, keeping his voice low so they weren't overheard. "That I was in love once and she ripped my heart out and tore it to pieces?"

Saffron blinked at him, but the expression on her face hardly changed. "You know what? I think this whole thing was a bad idea."

She stood and pushed back her chair, reaching for her purse.

"Saffron, wait." He jumped up and reached for her, one hand over her arm. "I'm sorry." What was he doing flying off the handle like that?

Her eyes were swimming with what he guessed was hurt or maybe just frustration. "This is crazy. I can't be this desperate," she murmured.

"I'm an idiot, and this isn't crazy. It's..." He shrugged. "Convenient. And it's going to work out just fine for both of us."

She looked unsure still, and he ran his hand down her arm until he could stroke her palm and then link fingers with her. He seriously needed to work on his bedside manner.

"Please. Just give me a chance. I promise I'll be better behaved."

Saffron slowly sat down again. Blake would bet there were eyes watching them, but he didn't care. He quickly ordered them champagne, then turned his full attention to Saffron. He sucked back a breath and forced himself to say the words.

"I was in love once, you were right. With a woman I wanted to spend the rest of my life with," he admitted, knowing that if he didn't do something, he was going to end up losing the woman he needed right now. Talking about his past wasn't something Blake made a habit of, and for ten years he hadn't shared what had happened with another soul. He cleared his throat. "Her name was Bianca, and we'd been together for three years. We met in school, and we were joined at the hip from that day on. I thought it was true love, or as true love as it can be when you're barely eighteen and haven't had a load of experience. I would have done anything for her, she was the love of my life."

Saffron's eyes were wide as she listened. "What happened to her?"

"Well," Blake said, nodding his thanks when their champagne arrived and reaching for the glass stem to worry between his forefinger and thumb, "we were off to college and planning our future, and I proposed to her. She said yes, we had crazy good sex, like we always did, and barely three weeks later she disappeared."

"What do you mean, disappeared?"

Blake held up his glass to clink against hers, taking a long sip. He wasn't big on bubbles, but they were supposed to be celebrating their engagement, and Saffron had seemed to enjoy the Veuve Clicquot the night before.

"She broke my heart," he said simply, still feeling the sting of betrayal. Not so much from her as from his father. "I searched for her. My father looked on, and eventually he admitted that he'd offered her money to leave. To not go through with the engagement."

"Your dad did that to you? You must have hated her for taking it!"

"I hated them both," Blake said honestly. "I already disliked my father, knew the moment I confronted him that it had been his doing. He never thought she was good enough for me—her family was not highly regarded or wealthy enough. But she was my girlfriend, the most important person in my life, the one person I was myself with and loved unconditionally." Blake leaned back. "My dad told me he'd known all along she was using me for our money, and he said all he'd done was prove he was right, that he hadn't actually done anything wrong. His theory was that she'd be knocked up within months just to make sure she had me trapped, well and good." He grunted. "Turns out the old man was right after all, although it didn't make me hate him any less. It was a lesson in love for me, and right then and there I decided it was going to be my last."

Saffron stroked his hand, her arm covering the space between them as she touched him. "Do you still love her?"

Blake laughed, but even to him it sounded cruel, dark. "No, sweetheart, I don't still love her. It was a decade ago now, and all it did was show me that the only person in life I could trust was myself."

"Do you still believe that?" she asked, leaving her hand on his as she sipped her champagne. "After all this time?"

He shifted so their connection was lost, disturbed by how easy their touch was. "I trusted my men when I was serving and the pilot sitting to my left, but I've never trusted another woman since."

She nodded, as if she understood, but he doubted she could. "I've only had one proper relationship."

"Hard to believe," he joked. "I could imagine you having suitors lined up for you backstage."

Her smile was cute, almost bashful. "It wasn't for lack of interest, but I just haven't had time. Work meant everything to me, right from when I was at high school, so it just never happened. Until I met Raf, a dancer I was paired with…"

Blake lifted his glass and she did the same. He waited for her to continue, not wanting to push. He knew how hard opening up was; he was still wondering what he'd just done by telling her about his past. But if they were going to make this work, make the next twelve months bearable, it had to be done.

"I fell hard for him, thought what we had was special. But he was sleeping with every other dancer behind my back. I felt stupid and ashamed, and when I ended it, he made me feel like I was the problem, not him." She shrugged, but the casual action didn't match the emotion he could see on her face, in her eyes. "I decided then and there I was better on my own, and I haven't let myself even come close to being hurt ever since."

"Here's to keeping our hearts safe," Blake said, holding up his glass.

"I'll drink to that," she agreed.

"You see, we're both proof that what we're doing is for the best."

"Yeah, maybe," Saffron muttered.

Blake wasn't sure he liked the fact he'd been

so open, but he'd told her now and it wasn't as if he could take it back.

"Let's order, and no more talking about exes," Saffron said.

Blake couldn't have put it better if he'd tried.

CHAPTER FIVE

"SO HERE WE are again."

Saffy shivered, even though the apartment was perfectly warm. She'd already discarded her leather jacket, so her arms were bare, but she felt exposed, as if she was naked. Blake's words were having an effect on her all over again; the only difference was that tonight she'd only had one glass of champagne, so she couldn't even blame the alcohol.

"Blake, can I ask you something?"

She watched as he threw his jacket down over the sofa and crossed the room, reaching for a bottle of whiskey.

"Did you know who I was when we met last night?"

He was frowning when he looked up. "No. I

was bored, and you were the most interesting person in the room."

She had no other choice but to believe him. Saffy was about to say something else when he turned with two tumblers and moved toward her. "I want to make it very clear that you deserve someone amazing one day, a man who'll love you like every decent woman deserves to be loved. I'm not that guy to any woman, but I will treat you well while we're under contract."

Even though she'd known exactly what she'd signed up for, had her eyes wide-open, the truth of their agreement still stung when he said it like that. It hurt that she was good enough for sex but not a real relationship, even though she understood his reasons. She was being sensitive, but knowing that didn't make it any easier to deal with.

She took the glass he passed her. "So is this to celebrate our twenty-four-hour anniversary?" she asked.

Blake's smile made his already perfect face

appear even more handsome. It softened his features, made her yearn to touch him and be in his arms again.

"Here's to us," he said, voice silky smooth. "I never break a contract, and I never back down on what I say. So I'll put good money on it that you'll be up and dancing again once you've had access to the best specialists money can buy."

She wished she could be as optimistic, but she knew firsthand that no matter how much money she had behind her, it wouldn't be easy. It gave her a better chance, but it didn't guarantee anything.

"And all I have to do is be the model wife, right?" She was only half joking, although she had no intention of giving a Stepford wife a run for her money.

"Don't lie to me, play the part when I need you to and we can coexist happily."

They stood facing each other, and Saffron held up her glass, clinking it to his and sipping when he did. The liquor was like silk in her mouth and fire in her throat, and when she swallowed her eyes burned. She blinked the tears away, not liking how amused Blake looked.

He laughed. "*More* than happily."

"I won't lie to you," she said honestly. "All I want to do is dance, and if you can give me that back, then I'll owe you everything." It was the pure, raw truth. There wasn't much she wouldn't do to get her dream back, and even though she was so close to losing hope, she would not stop fighting until the bitter end.

"Come here," he said gently.

Saffy hesitated, waited, wasn't sure if she wanted to give in to the way she was feeling just yet. Until Blake reached for her. His fingers closed over her arm, then worked their way up, each movement sending shivers through her body that she couldn't control. Her mouth parted as he slid his body forward, moved into her space, his body just grazing hers.

"I don't want to presume anything. I mean, anything we do for real has to be your choice."

Saffy stared up at him, eventually nodded. "Uh-huh," she whispered back. She liked that he wasn't pushing her, that the ball was in her court.

"It's your choice," Blake said softly, his eyes full of concern. "I have a perfectly nice spare bedroom with its own bathroom that I haven't even showed you yet, or you could just move into my room with me. We'd need to keep most of your things in my room, though, because I don't want my housekeeper being suspicious, or anyone else who might come over."

Saffron gulped, her eyes fixed on his mouth, carefully pressing her lips to his when he kissed her again, slipping her free arm around his neck to draw him even closer. He was magnetic and handsome and sexy…and technically he was hers. And she did want to be in his room. Besides, her excuse could be that she didn't think the housekeeper would buy their marriage as real if the sheets in the spare room were always rumpled.

When Blake finally pulled back it was to down the rest of his whiskey and discard his glass, placing it on the coffee table and turning back to her with a smile that made her think of only one thing. For a girl who was always so focused and made the right decisions, she was ready to make a bad one all over again very quickly.

"What do you say, fiancée?" he asked.

Saffron bravely sipped her drink, the burn just as bad this time as the first. "I say I haven't had much to make me smile these last few months. Why not?"

Blake took her hand and led her to his room. They stopped only for him to flick off the lights, bathing the apartment in darkness. The only light was from the bedside lamps in his room.

What she was doing was so out of character, but for some crazy reason it felt all kinds of right. Thankfully the awkwardness of earlier had faded a little.

When they reached the bedroom, Blake stood

in front of her, kissing her again before gently slipping the strap on her dress down and covering her bare shoulder with his mouth.

If only it was real. She couldn't help her thoughts, even as she tried to push them away. Part of it was real, surely, but the other part...he might not want to date her, or marry her, but his hands on her body and the look in his eyes told her that his desire for her was definitely real.

"Blake, I..." Saffron groaned, not wanting to ruin the moment but needing to.

"What is it?"

"I just, I need you to know why I said yes."

"Right now?" he asked, eyebrows raised.

She nodded, reaching for his hand. Suddenly she needed to tell him, had to get it off her chest so he understood who she was.

"Talk to me," Blake said, pulling her over to sit beside him.

Saffy sighed. "When I was younger, I had an operation for cervical cancer. I've known since I was nineteen that I couldn't have children, so I want you to know that's something you don't need to worry about with me." It wasn't something she usually shared, except with other women to encourage them to have regular checkups, but she wanted Blake to know. She knew how lucky she was to be alive, and it had been the only other time in her life that she'd had a break from dancing. Although that had been a very short one, and it hadn't had any impact on her career, as she'd simply been declared injured for a month.

"I'd always imagined my future with kids in it, once I'd fulfilled my career ambitions, but since that happened I've focused on dancing being my future. I need to dance, because it's the only part of my future I feel I can have any control over."

"I get it," he said. "I'm sorry for what you went through."

"Thanks," she whispered, dropping her head to his shoulder.

"So you can't ever get pregnant, or it's unlikely?"

"Can't ever," she said. "So you've got no worries with me. Besides, I couldn't ever dance the hours I need to and be a mom, so it's not that big a deal to me anymore." Saffron could joke about it now, but at the time she'd mourned the children she would never have, and even joking about it still stung deep down. She'd been too young at the time to want to be a mother then and there, but when the possibility was taken away it had still cut deep, because it had changed the future she'd imagined for herself. But then she'd simply thrown herself back into ballet and tried never to think about it again.

"Come here," Blake murmured in a low tone that sent a delicious shiver down her spine. He pulled her closer, facing her now.

She loved the gruff way he spoke to her, tugging her hard against him.

"Kiss me again," Saffron whispered, forcing herself to be bolder, to ask for what she wanted.

She wanted to forget about everything she'd just told him now she'd gotten it off her chest.

Blake didn't disappoint. His lips crushed her, hands skimming her body as she looped her arms around his neck. As far as forgetting all her troubles, this was exactly what she needed. Short-term, fun, mind-blowing…the perfect interlude while she focused on her body and got back her strength.

As she used her toes to push herself forward, climb up closer to him, she couldn't help the grin that took over her mouth.

"What?" Blake muttered.

"It didn't hurt," she whispered back, flexing her toes and her legs again.

"What? My kissing you?"

"My leg, stupid." Saffy didn't want to talk about it, but her lack of pain when she'd put that kind of pressure on her pointed toes had sent another kind of thrill through her.

Saffron woke and reached out in the bed. She didn't connect with anything. She sat up and searched in the dark for Blake, but the only thing she saw was a sliver of light coming through the door from the living room.

She stretched and got up, still tired but feeling restless. It was weird waking up in Blake's apartment, feeling like a visitor yet knowing she was here to stay. She pulled on the shirt he'd discarded earlier, wrapping it around herself and padding across the thick carpet. The light that she'd seen was a lamp in the far corner of the living room. The light was bathing part of the apartment in a soft light, and she could see the back of Blake's head. She guessed he might be working, unable to sleep and putting his time to good use, but when she reached him, bending down to run her hands down his bare chest from behind, she saw he was staring at a photograph.

"Oh," she stammered.

Blake jumped, dropping the photo.

"I'm sorry. I thought you'd be working, or reading a book or something. I just…"

Saffy didn't know what to say. She looked away as he brushed his knuckles against his eyes, knew that she'd been right in thinking she'd seen tears glinting there. She'd interrupted what was definitely supposed to be a private moment.

"Are you okay?" she asked.

"No," he ground out, sitting deeper into the buttoned leather armchair again and wearing only his boxers.

"Was that…?" She had been about to ask if it was his dad before his blank look silenced her.

"Go back to bed," he said.

Saffron watched him for a moment, thought about pushing the point, then did as he said. He might appear carefree, as though he was in control of everything in his life, but Blake had demons. She'd just seen them firsthand, sitting there in the dark alone, and she knew there was more to her husband-to-be than met the eye. He was acting the part of the happy bachelor, but she didn't believe it for a second.

And he wasn't alone. Tears pricked her eyes as she closed the bedroom door behind her and flopped back onto the bed, pulling the covers up and wishing it were her room and she wouldn't have to face him again. There was so much she had locked away, hidden so deep within herself that she would never open up to anyone. Only she was better at hiding it than Blake, because she'd just glimpsed his soul and his hurt looked a lot closer to the surface than she would ever let hers be.

She pulled a pillow closer, hugged it tight and buried her face into it. If only she could dance again, then everything would be okay. And she wouldn't have to stay here if things turned weird and she wanted out.

Blake felt terrible. He wanted to roar like a lion, yell about the injustices in the world and smash something. Slam his fist into a wall. But instead he stayed silent, lived with the guilt that was weighing on him like a ton of bricks, pushing down so hard on him that he could hardly breathe. He wasn't the angry type, which was why he was beating himself up so much right now.

It always happened at night. He'd go to sleep, fall into a deep slumber, then wake in the darkness, a tangle of sheets and sweat. If it wasn't his father, the helicopter wreckage, doubling over when he saw his brother's mangled body, it was the carnage he'd seen when serving. And that's why it affected him so badly. When he'd been away, he'd been able to compartmentalize the horrors, put his memories into a little box that he'd mostly managed to keep a lid on. But seeing his father and brother dead, like casualties of war among the pieces of metal covering the grass and strewn through trees, had changed everything. Because now images of war, memories he'd once buried, were merging with fresher ones, morphing into visions that often took hours to push away, if he could at all.

Blake steeled his jaw, glanced over at the whiskey bottle but refused to get up and reach for it. He'd gone to sleep with a beautiful woman in his arms, felt at peace, but when he'd woken, his demons had returned stronger than ever.

He shouldn't have shut her down like that, but then he shouldn't have done a lot of things. Maybe everything was just catching up with him. Maybe he should have found new investors, cashed in the business. He could have left his family in a great financial position, provided more for his mother and sisters than they'd ever need, but he was too loyal, too proud or maybe just too stubborn to give up what his family had built.

He shut his eyes, leaned back. His father had finally managed to turn him into the puppet he'd always wanted him to be, controlling him from the grave. All the years he'd fought with him, hated him, stood up to him, and now he just wished he was back. Then everything could go back to normal. That he could have his brother alive and kicking again. Because that was his biggest regret, falling out with the one person who'd have had his back no matter what, but whom he'd been too pigheaded to apologize to. Just another thing he'd never forgive himself for.

Blake doubted he'd find it easy to get back to sleep, and he also doubted Saffron would want him crawling in beside her. And what would he say to her? How could he even start to explain the way he felt? The things that haunted him were not things he wanted to burden anyone else with. Besides, they'd known each other less than two entire days. He wasn't about to crack his heart open and pour out all his feelings to her. Or to any woman. He'd already told her enough when he'd confessed about his ex.

Trouble was, he liked Saffron. And he hated the way he'd spoken to her. Because behaving like that only made him like his father, and he'd rather jump off a bridge than turn into even a shadow of his dad.

He picked up the photo of his father and brother he'd been holding, stared into his brother's eyes one last time, remembering his smile, how passionate he'd been about helicopters and taking over their dad's corner office one day. How good he'd been at schmoozing clients and smoothing over problems. Problems that peeved Blake, first world issues that drove him nuts. After what he'd seen, the things he'd had to do to protect his country, to serve, they weren't real problems in his eyes. Their clients, who were worth millions, hired and leased Goldsmith's helicopters and private planes. They'd made his family a whole lot of money, and his father had been well-known among New York's elite—*America's* elite. But that man, that smiling face that everyone else saw, wasn't the true man. Which might have been half the reason Blake had never been able to smile himself unless he truly meant it.

He tucked the photo into a book and switched off the lamp, staring out the window for a while.

New York was the city that never slept, and he was starting to be the guy who never slept. The fatigue was killing him, but somehow a few strong coffees always seemed to give him enough energy to get through the following day. *Just*.

Saffron had a sick feeling in her stomach when she woke. She kept her eyes shut, this time hoping that Blake wouldn't be there when she slowly slid her fingers across the sheets. She peeked out, breathing a sigh of relief when she found she was alone. Again.

She got up, walked into the bathroom and re-trieved the robe she'd left in there, tucking her-self up in it. Then she summoned all the bravery she could and walked out, expecting to find Blake asleep on the sofa. Instead, she discov-ered him standing in the kitchen, bare chested and staring intently at something.

"Morning," she called out, surprised by how

normal her voice sounded when she was a bundle of nerves.

Blake was frowning when he looked up, but his face quickly transformed into a smile when he saw her. "Morning."

She wasn't sure what else to say, whether they were just going to pretend nothing had happened or whether she should bring it up.

"I'm trying to make you breakfast," he said. "And for a guy who's used to ordering in, it's not as easy as it sounds."

She relaxed a little. "What are you making over there?"

His smile encouraged her to go a little closer. "Waffles again. I was given this fancy maker and I've never used it, so here goes."

Saffron laughed. "First of all, you don't need to keep feeding me. I'll never be a ballerina again if I keep eating with you." She was going to lean over the counter but decided to go around instead. "Second, you just whisk up the batter and pour it in. It ain't rocket science."

"You've making me feel like an idiot," he said with a chuckle. "I can fly a helicopter, but I can't use a whisk."

"You can?"

He gave her a quick sideways glance. "Yeah. It's what I've been doing most of my life."

Saffron tried to hide her surprise. Instead she leaned over and checked out the batter. "You're doing okay, just keep whisking until the lumps are out and give it a go."

Blake turned his attention to her, and she found it hard to read his expression.

"I'm not good at apologies, but I shouldn't have been such an idiot last night."

She appreciated he was trying to say he was sorry. "It's fine. I didn't mean to sneak up on you. I had no idea…"

He shook his head. "Let's just forget it. Okay?"

She nodded. "Okay."

There was something so magnetic about him, a feeling that pooled in her belly whenever she was with him. And seeing him standing in his jeans, bare chested with all his sinewy muscles on display, only reminded her all over again of how much fun she'd had in his bed. Even if she was still cautious after the way he'd reacted.

It was as though they were playing some silly cat-and-mouse game, only she didn't quite have a grasp of the rules yet.

She decided to make coffee instead of ogling his gorgeous body. "Coffee?" she asked, realizing she had no idea how he liked it.

"Love one. Black with one sugar."

Saffy busied herself, keeping her back turned even though she was still crazy aware of him. She got that he had issues, and she'd been so hurt last night, but they hardly knew each other and they were suddenly living together. It was never going to be easy.

"Here we go," she said, spinning around and just about slamming into him. She hadn't been expecting him to be just standing there.

"Thanks." He held out a hand to steady her, smiled down at her with his dreamy dark eyes.

She really needed to get back to work! It wasn't like her to be so taken with a man, and she was blaming it on not having anything else to think about.

Blake didn't pull away immediately, and she held her breath, gazing back at him. She was also starting to blame not getting this sort of thing out of her system on when she was younger. The excitement of what they were doing felt forbidden because it was so different from her usual behavior.

She smelled something that didn't seem quite right. "I think your waffle is burning."

Blake spun around, sloshing his coffee and making her laugh. "All I had to do was wait for the green light to come on. Who could burn a freaking waffle?"

Saffy perched on the bar stool so she could watch him. "Just throw it out. The next one will be perfect."

He muttered something and did what she'd

suggested. Her stomach rumbled as he poured more batter in.

"So what would a normal Sunday look like for you?" she asked.

"Honestly?" he said, hands flat on the counter as he leaned forward. "I'd probably be eating breakfast that I'd ordered from downstairs, then I'd be heading in to the office for a bit. Maybe going to the gym. You?"

She watched as he removed the first waffle and put it on a plate. He pushed it along the counter and passed her the maple syrup.

"If I was dancing, I'd be there around ten. My breakfast would probably be a protein shake instead of something like this, because I'd be being a lot more careful with my weight!"

"So you always worked on a Sunday?" he asked.

She cut into the waffle, slicing the first heart-shaped piece apart. "We only had Mondays off, and even then I'd be doing something work related. Although I always tried to get a massage in the afternoon." A wave of nostalgia hit her, just like it always did when she talked about dancing. "Every other day of the week I'd be in the studio by ten, and I'd be dancing or doing dancing-related things until around seven each night, unless we were performing, and then it'd be closer to eleven."

Blake whistled. "I had no idea the hours were so long."

She grimaced. "It's a killer, especially when you first start, but I love it. I would do it until I was sixty if I could."

"So tell me what happened," he said, voice suddenly a whole lot gentler. "I can see how much it hurts for you to talk about."

"I want to talk about that as much as you want to open up to me," Saffy said honestly.

Blake flipped out another waffle, stayed silent, although it wasn't awkward this time. She ate a few mouthfuls of her waffle, loving the drizzle of maple syrup.

"This is great," she praised him.

He smiled and passed her another, even though she stuck her hand out to protest.

"No more!" she managed when she'd finished her mouthful.

Blake just grinned and kept cooking.

"We were performing *Swan Lake*, and I was the lead. It had been amazing, night after night of great reviews," Saffron told him, suddenly needing to get it all out, to just tell him and get it over with instead of keeping it all bottled up inside. "I've had a lot of problems with a form of arthritis since I was young, and I was probably pushing myself too hard. That night I ripped three ligaments in my leg, which was bad enough without the crippling arthritis in my knee."

Blake looked up at her but didn't say anything, and she didn't want him to. There was nothing he could say that would make it any better.

"When I was in the army, I flew helicopters every day, doing what I loved," he said in a quiet voice, not making eye contact, just staring at the waffle machine. "I'd butted heads with my dad for years, but I wasn't going to back down on doing what I was passionate about. I wanted to make a difference, and I wanted to do something that made me feel great. The types of helicopters I was flying, dropping Navy SEALs into remote locations, being part of the most incredible teams…" He paused. "It was the best job in the world."

Saffron forced herself to keep eating, knowing how hard it was to share when every word felt so raw. Maybe that was why she was so drawn to Blake, because even though they were so different, they'd both lost what they loved. It wasn't a person they'd lost, but the pain was so real, so true, that Saffy felt every day as if her heart had been ripped out. She got it.

"Last night, you saw me looking at a photo of my dad." She listened to him take a deep, shaky breath. "And my brother."

"You lost them, didn't you?" she asked quietly. He nodded. "Yeah, I did. And as much as I miss my brother, so bad, I feel like it was just one more way for my dad to force me into what he always wanted me to do. Another way for him to control me. I know it sounds stupid, but in the middle of the night that's all I can think about."

Saffron wanted to reach for him, but she didn't know if it was the right thing to do or not. When he joined her at the counter and poured syrup over his waffles, she turned to face him, coffee cup in hand.

"We just have to cope as best we can, right?" she said. "It's so hard to make a career from doing what you love, and when that gets taken away…"

"It's heartbreaking," he muttered. "But yeah, you've just got to grit your teeth and keep on going. What other choice do we have?"

They sat side by side and finished their breakfast, and Saffron rose to rinse the plates and put them in a dishwasher.

"What do you say we go ring shopping?" Blake asked, taking her by surprise.

She tried to hide her grin. Ring shopping sounded like a lot more fun than her usual Sunday afternoon, and she liked the idea of getting out of the apartment. "Give me an hour. A girl's got to look good for that kind of outing."

"You always look good."

Saffy paused, heard what Blake had muttered. She was going to say something, but her brain was blank. Instead she closed the dishwasher door and headed for the bathroom. When she got there, she did what she always did in the mornings, lifting her right leg high and placing it on the edge of the bathroom cabinetry to stretch out her muscles. The granite in Blake's bathroom was cold against her skin, but it felt nice and she let her body fall down, the burn of her muscles making her feel alive. She lifted up then down again before repeating the stretch on the other side, the movement as natural to her as brushing her teeth.

Once she was finished she stared back at her reflection, checked her posture. She would always be a dancer. Every fiber in her body told her it wasn't over yet, and this morning her determination to listen to that feeling was back tenfold.

CHAPTER SIX

"WHAT DO YOU THINK?" Blake asked as they walked through the door of the antique jeweler his mother had always favored.

Saffron's eyes seemed to twinkle when she looked up at him, holding his hand. He'd linked their fingers as they'd headed through the door, conscious of how they appeared together, and somehow it felt right. He was oddly comfortable around Saffron most of the time, more himself than he probably was around even his family. Maybe because he'd laid it all out on the line with her, been honest from the get-go because of the kind of relationship they were in.

"I was expecting Tiffany's," she said.

"We can go there if you want."

"No," she said, letting go of his hand to peer

into a display cabinet. "I didn't say I didn't like it—it's amazing. Besides, beggars can't be choosers, right?"

He laughed and watched as she wandered around, smiling to the assistant when she came over.

"Can I help you?"

"Yes," Blake said. "I'm looking for something for my fiancée here. Something elegant."

They started to look, with the assistant showing them a few engagement rings.

"Sir, is there any price range I need to be mindful of?" she asked in a hushed tone.

Blake smiled, reaching out for Saffron. "No. Whatever she wants."

Saffron shot him a look, and he just raised an eyebrow and smiled back at her. He was enjoying the charade more than he'd expected to.

"How about this one?" Saffron asked, pointing to a solitaire diamond surrounded by smaller ones, with baguette diamonds on each side forming the band.

The ring was beautiful and no doubt expensive, but he admired the fact she hadn't just chosen the largest, since he'd already told her she could keep it when their charade was over.

"Try it on," he instructed.

When the assistant passed it over, he quickly grabbed it, changing his mind. "Let me," he said.

Saffron turned to face him, and he smiled as he dropped to one knee in the store. "Saffron, will you marry me?" he asked, wanting to see her smile, knowing it would make her happy even though they weren't marrying for real.

They had talked about marriage, about what they were doing, but he hadn't actually proposed to her. Until now.

She held out her hand, letting him slip the ring on. "Yes," she whispered, laughing at him.

The shop assistant clapped as Blake rose and dropped a gentle kiss to her lips, liking how soft and warm her mouth was against his. It wasn't as though kissing her was a hardship.

"We'll take it," he said when he finally pulled away, reminding himself that it wasn't real, no matter how good Saffron felt against him.

The lines between fact and fiction were blurring between them, or maybe they'd always been blurred. The attraction between them was real; he just had to remember that it couldn't become—*wouldn't* become—anything more. It wasn't part of his plan, the future he imagined for himself, and there was no way he'd ever want a wife or a family. The example his father had set for him was testament to that. Besides, there would never be a woman he could trust enough with his heart or his money, and if he couldn't truly be himself without trying to protect himself and his family's fortune, then he'd never marry for real.

Once they'd paid for the ring, they left the shop with it on her finger.

"Well, that wasn't too hard," he said as they walked hand in hand down the sidewalk.

"It's beautiful," she said.

"And it's yours," he replied.

Saffron laughed as she leaned into him, still holding his hand. "It feels weird. I'm so girly and excited over the bling, but then this whole thing isn't real. I feel like I'm living someone else's life."

"Ditto," he said. Only he'd felt like that well before Saffron had come along. Every day he felt as if he was playing a role, one that had been destined for his brother, and he hated it. Every single day, he hated it.

"When we get back, I'll give you my planner to take a flick through. Anything marked social you'll need to attend with me, and I'll let you know in advance of any client dinners if I want you to join me."

Saffron looked up from admiring her ring. "Good. And I'll let you know how I do searching for specialists and treatments. There's an acupuncturist who works with celebrities I'd love to get in with, so I might need you to make the appointment!"

"I'll issue you a credit card tomorrow," Blake said, unworried, thinking through the logistics of everything. "That way you can pay for any medical expenses. Sound okay?"

She grasped his hand even tighter, but Blake didn't mind. "You've given me hope again, Blake. Just keep me in New York and I'll be the best wife you could have wished for."

He didn't doubt it.

"Oh, did I mention I want you to quit your job?" He'd forgotten all about telling her, but the last thing he wanted was for her to go back to pouring coffee. She could be a resting ballerina, holed up in his apartment or doing whatever she wanted, but he didn't want her tied to a job that she didn't even care about. If she was his wife, he would keep her and make sure she was available whenever he needed her. Besides, no one would believe in their marriage if he let Saffron work for minimum wage.

"You're serious?" Saffron asked, giving him a

look that made him realize she actually thought he was joking.

"Deadly," he replied. "No one would believe you were my wife if I let you slave away nine to five."

He saw a hesitant look pass over her face that made him wonder if she didn't like the idea of him keeping her. "Okay," she said. "I guess if you were my husband that's what you'd want."

Blake nodded, but her words jolted him. It was weird hearing her say the *husband* word, especially when in his mind he could still see his mother sobbing over something his father had done when he was only a child. They weren't blurry memories like so many of his childhood recollections, but a perfect snapshot of his mom crying that the man she'd married didn't deserve to be called her *husband*, the man who slammed the door and left her to cry.

He pushed the thoughts away and smiled down at the gorgeous redhead at his side. All the more reason to have a contract, to be clear up front about what he wanted.

Blake wasn't fit to be a real husband, didn't want that life. But he did want to be the one to step his family business into the future, wanted to make his family proud. Because if he wasn't so honorable, he'd have left and never looked back after the funeral, returning to the life he loved. Selfishly leaving everything behind to pursue his dreams, away from his family name and far away from New York. But that was the past now, and it wasn't something he could get back. *Ever.*

Oddly, he felt happier with Saffron at his side than he had for a long while. Or maybe it was just the promise of having her in his bed every night, and the fact he'd been honest with her about who he truly was.

"So this is the woman who got you all tied up in knots?" An elegant older woman with her hair pulled off her face stepped forward to collect

Saffron's hand. Her palm was warm, and even though she screamed old New York money, her smile was genuine.

"Mom, I'd like you to meet Saffron," Blake said, coming to her rescue and slinging an arm around her so he could pull her back.

"It's great to meet you," Saffron said, training a smile. "I've heard so much about you."

His mother's smile was wry, and it reminded Saffron of Blake. "I can't say the same about you. My son has been very tight-lipped about the beautiful woman he's all set to marry."

"Nothing fancy," Blake cautioned, taking Saffy's hand and pulling her toward him. She sat down on the sofa beside him, careful to curl up close, keeping a hand on his thigh. "Just a simple wedding."

He glanced down at her, and she retreated with her hand. The heat in his gaze was making her uncomfortable. This might be fake, but their chemistry wasn't, which was why she wasn't finding it that hard to pretend.

"When you say nothing fancy…?" his mother asked.

"I mean we're heading down to the registry office and signing the paperwork. No big ceremony, no fuss. You can wait until the girls get married for a big wedding, because I want this completely under the radar."

His mother pursed her lips, but Saffron could see she didn't want to argue with him, or maybe she knew from experience that there was just no point.

"Saffron, I don't want to offend you, but I must bring up the delicate subject of a prenuptial agreement."

Blake laughed and Saffron leaned into him. She'd been prepared for this, would have thought it odd if any mother with their kind of fortune hadn't raised an eyebrow at how quickly they were getting married.

"Please, Mrs. Goldsmith, that's not something you have to worry about. I have no intention of taking anything from your son or your family, and we've already organized the paperwork." Saffron chuckled. "But don't think for a moment I'm going to let your son run my life. I intend on having my career back on track very quickly. As soon as I've given my body a chance to rest and recover, I'll be back with the New York Ballet Company."

His mother smiled and looked to Blake. "I like her."

Blake dropped a kiss into her hair. It was just a casual, sweet gesture, but the gentleness of his touch took her by surprise.

"She's the one."

Saffron felt guilty sitting there, smiling away and pretending to dote on this woman's son. She seemed like a nice person, and lying wasn't something that came naturally to her, even if she was putting on a good show of doing exactly that right now. She wondered what it would be like if this were real, if she were actually being welcomed into the family. Saffron could see that she'd enjoy Blake's mother's company, which only made her guilt pangs stronger.

"You do realize the tabloids will stop hounding you. Not to mention it'll be good for business," his mother mused, shrugging into her coat and collecting her purse as they watched. "We should hold an engagement party for our clients, let them see what a family man you're becoming. What do you think?"

Blake stood, and she kept hold of him as she rose, too. "I think that sounds like a great idea. How about you organize it?"

His mother's smile was wide. "Excellent."

"Actually, maybe we should just start an annual party for our guests, and we can announce our marriage at this inaugural one to keep it low-key." He knew whom he wanted to impress, but it wouldn't do any harm to invite all their important clients.

Saffron nodded, listening and playing the part of attentive fiancée. She was used to playing a role as a dancer, to being in character, which was probably why this seemed easy. Or maybe Blake was just easy to be around. If she'd had to pick the kind of man she'd want to marry one day, it could have been him. *Maybe*. Although from what he'd said, he had no intention of ever marrying for real, never wanted to settle down.

And that was fine by her. Once she was dancing again, she'd have no time for a husband anyway. Blake would be a distant memory, and hopefully a pleasant one.

"Please tell me you'll invite me to the ceremony," his mother said as they walked out her door.

"Maybe," Blake answered. "Let's see if Saffron survives meeting my sisters first. She might run for the hills before I get her to sign on the dotted line."

Blake laughed and she forced a chuckle. If only his mother knew that she'd already well and truly signed on the dotted line. She was bound to marry Blake, which meant they were as good as husband and wife already. Besides, they'd already decided that they were going to get married in secret as soon as the license came through.

CHAPTER SEVEN

SAFFRON WAS SMILING, and even though her happiness wasn't forced, she wasn't finding it easy to look happy. What was she doing? Blake was treating her like his actual wife, and aside from when he woke up in hot sweats during the night and didn't want to talk about it, everything seemed…good. *Real.* Not that she was under any illusions, but still, it was weird.

"Come on, let's go," Blake said, kissing her on the lips and holding their joined hands in the air. "You were great tonight."

"You sound like my choreographer," she said with a laugh, still smiling as the crowd watched them. She was well used to being the center of attention, and far from feeling unusual having her every move watched just because she was on a man's arm, she was getting a kick out of it. Usually she basked in the attention, full of pride that so many people were enjoying her creative outlet, a performance she'd put hours of her time, not to mention sweat and sometimes blood, into. This time she felt like an actress, and for some reason it didn't feel any less satisfying. "Or maybe my cheerleader."

"You're brilliant, has anyone ever told you that?" Blake swept her into his arms and out of the room. She was starting to get the feeling that he was enjoying the performance as much as she'd enjoyed putting it on.

Saffron didn't want their conversation to turn around to her dancing, so she let it go and didn't answer. They headed straight outside and into the waiting town car.

"I think they bought it," she said.

Blake leaned over and kissed her, his lips familiar to her now yet still making her body tingle. It would have been a much easier arrangement if they hadn't started out by being intimate, although given the way her body reacted to him, she was starting to wonder if they could ever have been platonic.

"I have some key accounts that have always referred to my dad every time we met, gone on about the roots of the company being a family business and questioning my commitment, or at least that's what it's seemed like," Blake said, settling back into the leather seat. "I don't know if a rival was trying to get to them and spinning rubbish, or if it was just the reputation they thought I had, but things felt fragile there for a little while. Marrying you has made all that go away, and after tonight, man. You seriously wowed my big investor. I definitely believe you can be my little star for the next while."

"So it's been worth it for you already?" Saffron asked.

He grinned. "Yes. You?"

"You've given me access to medical professionals I'd never have been able to afford to consult with," she said honestly. "And I'm still here.

I still have a shot. So yeah." Saffron laughed. "Marrying you hasn't been half-bad!"

The car ride was only short, and soon they were heading up to their apartment. It already felt like home for Saffron after two short weeks, or as home as anything ever felt to her. She wasn't used to spending a lot of time wherever she lived, and she'd been living out of a suitcase on and off for years. But she had some photos up, Blake had given up half his wardrobe space to her and her perfume lingered when she walked into their room.

"I'm just going to respond to some work emails. I'll be in bed soon."

Saffy undressed and put on a nightie, then padded into the bathroom to take her makeup off. She never took the luxurious space for granted, with its floor-to-ceiling tiles and beautiful fittings, and the oversize fluffy towels were her idea of heaven. Especially since he had the housekeeper come in twice a week, so she didn't even have to lift a finger to keep them that way.

The apartment was silent except for the low hum of the television—she was used to Blake having it on whenever he sat up and worked late, which was most nights. She lowered herself to the ground, relaxed into the splits and dropped her body down low, covering first one leg and then the other. Once she was done stretching, she stood and raised up, on tiptoe, smiling to herself as she leaned to each side, reached up high, before doing a little turn. The acupuncture had definitely helped, and even though she could have kept going until she collapsed, she was going to follow her new specialist's orders and only stretch her muscles like that for five minutes each evening and morning.

Still smiling, she curled up beneath the covers and flicked through a magazine before turning off the bedside lamp and closing her eyes. She was going to wait up for him, but they'd had late night after late night and...

Saffron woke up with a fright, sitting bolt upright, heart racing.

"No!"

She blinked in the darkness, eyes slowly adjusting, realizing that it was Blake who'd woken her. She instinctively pulled back, putting some space between them.

"Blake," she said, loudly, forcing her voice. "Blake!"

He groaned but didn't wake, pulled the sheets tighter around himself, thrashing out.

"Blake!"

His eyes opened, a flash of brightness that scared her for a moment until they locked on her. He sat up, disheveled and disoriented looking.

"Saffy?" His voice was hoarse as he pushed the covers down.

"You were dreaming. Are you okay?" she asked, hesitant. She didn't want to push him—they had a good thing going, and that didn't involve asking too many personal questions, going too deep, unless they had to.

"Same thing every time." Blake sighed. "Every single time."

Saffron tucked her knees up to her chin. "Your dad?" she asked.

Blake flicked his bedside lamp on. "Yeah. Always him. Always a weird, I don't know, collage of memories, I guess. Just a jumble of things all mashed together."

"Do you still wish you were serving?" she asked. It was a question that had been on her lips all week, wanting to ask but not knowing if he'd want to talk to her. "That you could go back, even though you have these dreams?"

"Yeah," he said, running his fingers through his hair, shutting his eyes as he leaned back into the headboard. "Or maybe I don't. I don't know. All I know is that I miss flying, miss having my own identity that isn't tied to my family. As hard as it was, I still miss it, want it."

"I'm not sure what would be harder—having a dream and never turning it into reality, or the feeling of having that dream snatched away

when you've already tasted the reality of it."
Saffron reached for Blake, her fingers crawling
the space between them until they connected
with his. At least they knew what it felt like, understood what the other had been through on a
level that no one else could.

"Having it taken away," he replied, squeez-
ing her fingers back. "Definitely having it taken
away."

"Or maybe we wouldn't have the same fire
burning in us if we hadn't tasted that reality,
that dream," she whispered. "Maybe we're still
the lucky ones, we just can't see it."

"Maybe." He groaned, and she wasn't sure if
it was from pain or the subject matter.

"Tell me what it was like, what you loved
about it," she asked, suddenly wide-awake, not
wanting to go back to sleep if he wanted to open
up to her, to talk.

"One day," he said. "One day I'll tell you all
about it. About the kick I got every time I put
a Black Hawk up in the air or took a unit to

safety in a Chinook. But not right now. I need some rest."

She knew he had issues, that whatever was troubling him needed to be dealt with, but as he kept reminding her, it wasn't her problem. She wasn't his real wife. She was more like a live-in mistress with extra benefits.

His problems were his. Her problems were hers. A year or two of fun. A year or two of great sex and parties. One year or maybe more to get her career back on track and have fun while she tried to find her way back to the top. It sure beat going home to serve coffee for the rest of her life at a diner and wishing for what she didn't have. At least this way, what she'd lost still felt as if it was within arm's reach. What she craved so badly was still a possibility instead of simply a memory of what could have been.

CHAPTER EIGHT

Three months later

SAFFRON SMILED UP at Blake, expertly running her fingers down his dinner jacket–clad arm. It wasn't hard to pretend she adored him, but the weird thing was reminding herself all the time that it wasn't *real*. They slept in the same bed, they went to parties and functions, and they put on a perfect show of being a real couple. Which they kind of were. Pity he was so darn irresistible.

A waiter passed and she took a glass of champagne. She held it for a while, listening to Blake talk business, before raising the glass to her lips. She went to sip but then recoiled as the bubbles hit her tongue.

"Excuse me," she said, stepping away from

Blake quickly and scanning for the restroom. Bile rose in her throat, and she forced it down.

"Are you okay?" Blake's dark brown eyes met hers, concern etched on his face. So far she'd never let him down once, but this time she needed to bolt. Fast.

Saffy just nodded and hurried as fast as her high heels would let her. Thankfully her leg was feeling great and she hadn't had any problems with her knee, so she was able to move fast. Otherwise she'd have been vomiting in the nearest corner!

She left her glass on a ledge in the bathroom and only just made it to a stall, holding her hair back as she threw up into the toilet. Her body felt burning hot then chilled, sweat beading across her forehead before her skin turned cold. What on earth had she eaten? Or had she caught the stomach flu?

"You okay in there, sweetheart?" A kind voice sounded out.

Saffron hadn't even noticed anyone else. She'd

been so desperate not to be sick out in the open that she'd just hurried straight on through. "Um, I think so," she managed to say back, trying to hold down everything else in her stomach, if there was even anything else left.

"You don't sound drunk, and you didn't look drunk, so either you've eaten something bad or you've got a little one on the way. Am I right?"

Saffron laughed. "Has to be bad food." Another wave of nausea hit, and she leaned forward again, trying hard to hold it down and failing.

The woman sounded closer this time when she spoke. "You're sure it's not a baby?"

Saffron sighed and leaned against the wall of the stall. Usually she was grossed out by any kind of public toilet, but the cool felt nice against her body when she pushed back, and it was a pretty posh tiled bathroom with fancy lights and wallpaper. She hoped it was clean. Besides, she didn't have any other choice.

"Can't be a baby," she replied with a sigh.

"Not for me." Saffron finally opened the door and came face to a face with a nice-looking lady dressed in a beautiful taffeta gown. Her gray hair was pulled up into an elegant do.

"I was sick as a dog when I had my boys. Thin as a whippet so nobody knew I was pregnant, and I threw up for months."

Saffron appreciated her concern, and it was nice to have someone to take her mind off how ill she felt. The nausea had passed now, only re-turning when she thought about the champagne she'd almost drunk. She usually had a cast-iron stomach, so it seemed strange.

"Saffy, you in here?" Blake's deep voice boomed through the restroom.

She cleared her throat. "Just a sec."

"I'll tell your man you're not well. You take your time."

Saffy pulled herself together, taking a mint from her purse and then walking over to the mirrors to check her face. She looked pale and gaunt, but the sick feeling had passed. After washing her hands, she went to find Blake.

"What's wrong?"

His eyes were searching her face, and she had to look away. The hardest part about being with Blake was trying not to fall in love with the man. They'd felt like a real team when she'd been at his side, meeting his new investor and his wife; when Blake had secured the investment, she'd fist pumped and squealed as if it was her deal that had come together!

"I started feeling all weird, sweats and nausea. I think I ate something bad."

He frowned and put his arm around her as they walked back out. "Let's head home."

"No, you stay," she insisted, looking away when a waiter passed. She couldn't stand the thought of alcohol or food. "Schmooze your clients, do your work and let me go. You don't need me here—they've already seen you're a doting husband if that's what you're worried about."

She'd meant to sound positive, but instead it had come out all wrong.

"Just because this isn't, ah—" he cleared his throat, frowning again "—doesn't mean I don't care about you."

Saffy squeezed his hand. "I know. I just meant that I've already fulfilled my purpose." She felt sick again and held his hand tight, waiting for it to pass. "I really have to go."

Blake let go of her hand and pulled out his phone. "Make your way out. I'll call the driver now and have him waiting for you."

Saffron smiled her thanks and hurried through the throng of people toward the exit. She kept her head down, not wanting to make eye contact and have to talk to anyone. She just wanted to undress and crawl into bed.

As promised the car was there within minutes of her walking outside, although she would have been happy to stand and gulp in the cold air for longer. She got in the vehicle and slumped on the backseat. As they headed for home she stared out the window, her hand resting on her stomach in an effort to calm it. It wasn't working, but she kept it there anyway.

Pregnant. She smiled despite how shaky she felt. There was no way she could be pregnant. The specialist had made it so clear to her, and she'd looked into freezing her eggs before having it done, but the success rates of thawing those frozen eggs hadn't seemed worth it to her, not when she'd been so short of money.

Pregnant. Was there even a slim chance? She'd only been with Blake that one time without protection, and if her chances of getting pregnant were statistically zero, surely it couldn't have happened...

"Pull over, please!" she cried as they passed a convenience store.

The driver did as she asked, pulling over farther up the block when it was safe and there was space to park.

"I'll only be a minute," she said, jumping out and rushing back. She entered the store and found the section with women's things, reaching for the first pregnancy test she could find. There were two types, so she grabbed the other one as well, hands shaking so hard she had to concentrate on getting her card out to pay.

"Thanks," she mumbled as she took her things and raced back to the car. It was only a short drive, but it seemed to take forever. When they pulled up outside she raced in, forgetting how ill she'd been. Saffy headed for the bathroom, not bothering to turn any lights on except the one she needed to. The rest of the apartment was dark, except for a couple of lamps, but she didn't care. All she wanted was to do the test so she could be sure that there was absolutely no chance of her being pregnant.

Saffy hovered above the toilet and held the stick out, counting to three before retrieving it. She put the cap back on it and placed it on the counter, staring at the tiny screen that would show one line if she wasn't pregnant. That line showed, strongly, and as she held her breath another faint line appeared, slowly but surely. *Two blue lines.* Nausea washed over her again, but this time she was sure it was from nerves. She couldn't be pregnant!

She paced around the bathroom for a few minutes then ripped open the wrapper on the other test. This one was more expensive, so she was sure it would be more accurate.

She'd only just been, but she forced herself to go again, to do just enough so that the test would work. And then she played the waiting game again, staring at the slightly bigger screen.

Pregnant. Just one word. One simple word.

And it changed everything.

CHAPTER NINE

SAFFRON CLUTCHED HER bag tight and walked back out onto the street. The day was warm and the sun was hot on her bare arms, but she hardly noticed. She just wanted to get to the studio where she'd been training.

Pregnant. She'd known the two home tests the night before couldn't be wrong, but still. After so many years of believing she could never be a mom, it was almost impossible to comprehend. And what was she going to tell Blake? Saffy groaned and held her bag tighter, scared of what was happening inside her, how much everything was changing.

She felt a vibration against her and realized it was her phone. She pulled it out, glancing at the screen and expecting it to be Blake, not ready to talk to him yet. But it was a number she didn't recognize.

She inhaled and stopped walking. "Hello, Saffron speaking."

"Saffron, it's Benjamin. From NYC Ballet."

Her heart just about stopped beating. "Oh, hi," she stammered.

"I wanted to know how you are. Whether you've had any success with your recovery?"

Saffy flexed her foot, something she always did whenever she thought about her injury or someone asked her about it. She couldn't help but smile when she did it without pain. "I'm doing really well. I've seen some great physical therapists, an acupuncturist and a specialist doctor, and I think I'm ready to ease back into dancing again."

It was a half lie, because the amazing people she'd been seeing had all told her to simply start exercising more, to slowly start dancing ten or so minutes a day after running through a series of stretches and strapping her leg. To try taking a few dance classes but not specifically ballet, and they'd been making her consume all types of natural wonder products in conjunction with the medicines the doctor had prescribed. The specialist had been incredibly helpful, referring her to the almost-impossible-to-get-in-with therapist in the first place. She'd already enrolled in modern dance, just to start using her muscles, but only ballet was going to fill the void she felt every day.

"That's fabulous news, darling," Benjamin said. "We all thought you might have gotten married and forgotten about us."

"Never," Saffron murmured. "Dance will always be the most important thing in my life."

He laughed. "Just don't let your new husband hear you talk like that!"

Saffron felt as though she was walking on ice, just teetering and waiting. Why had he phoned her? She was too scared to ask. There had to be a reason for a call to just come out of the blue after so long with no contact.

"Darling, the purpose of my call is to see if we can book you. It's not for another four months, but it's you we need." He cleared his throat. "Can you be ready by then? Are you planning on making a comeback?"

Saffy went burning hot then freezing cold, as if her body was going into shock. Four months? Her hand went instinctively to her stomach. In four months she was going to have a bump. A *very* big bump. If she had this baby, there was no way she'd be able to dance then, no matter how well her leg was holding out.

"Why me?" she asked.

"It's for Pierre. He's retiring from the company, and he's requested you as the dancer for his final show. It's just a one-off performance for him, to thank him for all the years he's put into our choreography, but it's you and only you he wants."

Saffron gulped. Pierre was the reason she'd been the lead in *Swan Lake*. Pierre had given her that big break, had believed in her and what her future could hold. Pierre was the key to her getting back on stage, because only he would request her and not take no for an answer.

"Can I have some time to think about it?" Saffron said, stalling, not ready to say no when she didn't even know what she was going to do, what the next few months of her life would even look like. "I'll need to talk to my physical therapist and specialist, make sure they don't think it's too soon. I don't want to risk injury again." She shook her head, wondering where the words were coming from. She wasn't even over her old injury yet!

"We love you here, Saffron," he said. "Take the week to think about it and let me know. If you do this, you'll be officially invited back to join the company. You were one of Pierre's best principal dancers, darling. We want you back home where you belong, and I just don't believe you're done yet."

Tears welled in Saffy's eyes. It was the phone call she'd been dreaming of, her big chance.

But even without the baby, she had no idea whether she'd ever be strong enough to be a principal again, not until she started training and saw firsthand if her leg tolerated the punishing hours.

"I'd do anything to be back. Trust me," she said, voice as shaky as her hands as she gripped her phone.

When she hung up, all she felt was emptiness. What she'd wanted was so close she could almost taste it, almost within her grasp. But then once upon a time, being a mother had seemed important, when the idea of being a parent had been taken from her. She'd been horrified at the time that she would never have children, something she'd slowly forgotten about the more she'd progressed in her career. But now… She slid her hand back down over her belly, the action seemingly normal now. She was suddenly protective of the little being growing inside her, even though she wasn't sure how she felt about the whole thing. *She was pregnant.*

She reached the studio and entered, pleased there was only one other dancer there running through a routine. She stripped down to her leotard and tights, carefully putting on her ballet shoes and looking down at her legs. She warmed up by stretching out slowly, trying not to think, trying to just focus on what she was about to do, on dance. She lifted a leg carefully into the air, stretched up, rose up then down, using the barre, feeling her muscles as they pulled then released. When she had both feet back on the ground, she stretched some more before leaving the barre to dance a quick routine, to cross the room once, dancing like she used to, dancing in a way that used to come as naturally as breathing to her.

And it still did. Breathless but not in pain, Saffy stopped, knew she had to. If she had it her way she would dance all day, but she wasn't ready. Not physically.

After warming down, stretching some more, she slipped her yoga pants back on and then her sweater, collecting her bag and heading back out the door. Saffy set off at a walk, heading for the apartment, needing to face reality. Either she told Blake and he would deal with it, let her make her own decision about what to do, or she never let him find out. He didn't want to be a dad—he'd made that clear when they'd signed the marriage contract—and she'd told him outright that her getting pregnant was impossible. He'd just think she was a liar, that she'd purposely deceived him, set out to fool him. This didn't have to be his problem; it was something she could deal with on her own. If she wanted this baby, she could do it. Trouble was, she'd signed a marriage contract, and she knew Blake only had one of the deals together that he'd needed her for, and she doubted he'd want to let her out of the contract so easily. Not until he had what he needed from their arrangement.

She let herself in and went straight for the kitchen, pouring a big glass of water and drinking it down. Then she peeled a banana and sat in silence, eating.

"Saffy?"

She jumped, choking on her mouthful. What was Blake doing home?

"Blake?" Saffy walked toward the bedroom. "Where are you?"

"In bed. I'm sick," he said.

She peeked in. "I had no idea you were here."

"I think I've got the stomach flu that you had," Blake said, groaning. "Where have you been?"

It was an innocent question, but it felt like an interrogation all of a sudden. Because for once she'd been somewhere she shouldn't have. "Um, just the doctor," she told him, going closer and sitting down on the bed beside him, reaching for his hand. It was warm, his skin comforting against hers. "I've been thinking about going back to the studio some more, actually pushing my leg a little to see how I do, see if I'm ready to go back."

His smile was kind, and he let go of her hand

to prop himself up on the pillows. They'd developed a relationship that went way beyond a simple contract, an easiness that she would miss. Blake was complicated yet beautiful, a man who was straight up about what he wanted, but one who was hiding a power load of pain. He'd shared so little with her about how he truly felt, had just scratched the surface and told her the bare bones of his past, but she knew how much he hurt, how hard it was for him to trust. And now she had to figure out how to tell him what had happened, make him believe that she hadn't deceived him.

"What happened?" he asked, staring into her eyes like he always did and making her feel as if she was the only person in the room, as though what they had was genuine. As real as it felt sometimes.

Heat started to rise up her body, flooding her cheeks. This time she had to lie. "I had a phone call. An opportunity."

"To dance again?" he asked.

Saffy nodded. "Yes. In four months' time, if I'm up to it."

"That's great news," Blake said with a smile. "I'd offer to celebrate with you, but…"

She held up her hand and rose. "I'll let you rest."

Saffron was relieved to walk away and not have to talk more, because she had a lot of thinking to do. More than that, she needed to make a decision. The doctor had been very diplomatic in explaining all her options, but the thought of anything other than protecting the growing baby inside her made her want to be physically sick. But what if this was her one and only chance to dance again? What if this was the last time in her life she'd be offered an opportunity like this? What if…

Saffy bit down hard on her lip. *Be a mother.* She collapsed onto the sofa, finding it hard to breathe. *Or be a dancer.*

She dug her nails into the cushion beside her. *Run away from Blake and never look back.*

Right now, it was sounding like the best option. Or maybe it was feeling like her only option. She couldn't give up this baby, which meant she couldn't be a dancer, not now, maybe not ever, because Pierre would be gone and then she'd have to try to impress a new choreographer who didn't know or love her. Besides, the two didn't go hand in hand, not with the hours she'd have to dedicate to dancing again *if* her body ever let her. And there was no way she could dance that punishing routine at all during pregnancy, not a chance.

Blake checked his watch and frowned at the time. It was unusual for Saffron to be so late. He was going to wait another five minutes but changed his mind, leaving a tip on the table and simply walking out. He wasn't that hungry anyway, and he wanted to make sure she was okay.

He dialed her number and it went straight to voice mail. Again.

Blake left a message this time. "Hey Saffy, it's

me. We had a dinner reservation at seven—did you forget? I'm on the way home now. We can always order something in. Call me."

It didn't take him long to make it back, and when he let himself in, something felt wrong.

"Saffy?" he called. When she didn't answer he headed straight for the bedroom. Maybe she was in the shower. "Saffron?"

And then he stopped. There was no five-book-high pile on her bedside table, no perfume bottles or jewelry scattered on the buffet beneath the big mirror. He walked faster into the bathroom. No makeup, no hairspray, no deliciously citrus smell.

Blake stopped dead in front of the closet, not hesitating to yank the doors open and stare inside. The empty space hit him like a fist to his gut. What was going on?

Saffy was gone. She was gone as though she'd never existed in the first place, as if she'd been a figment of his imagination.

Just like Bianca. Just like the day he'd found their little apartment empty all those years ago.

He walked backward until his legs touched the bed, and he dropped down on to it, not noticing the cream envelope until he was sitting. He slipped his finger beneath the seal and plucked out the single piece of paper inside, unfolding it and instantly recognizing Saffron's handwriting.

Blake,

I left like this because I didn't want to look you in the eye and tell you the truth myself. The last few months might have been an arrangement, but I feel closer to you than I ever really have to any other person before. And that's why I didn't want to see the distrust in your eyes when you found out that I was pregnant. You deserved to know, but you don't owe me anything. This baby suddenly means the world to me, and I'll do everything I can to make this little person be loved. I'm sorry I left when I was supposed to stay with you as your wife for longer, but staying would have only made things more complicated. You made it clear that you never wanted a family, or a real wife, and the last thing I want to do is trap you into something else you don't want.

I've kept the ring only because you told me it was mine, and it'll help tide me over until I can work again.

I'm sorry things had to end this way, and I want you to know that you'll always hold a special place in my heart. Don't try to find me, just let me go.

Saffron

What the... Blake screwed up the letter into a tight ball and threw it across the room. She was *pregnant*?

He rose and stormed into the kitchen, wrapping his hand around a bottle of whiskey and pouring a big splash into a glass. He knocked it straight back.

Pregnant? How? They'd always used protection. Besides, she'd told him she couldn't have children, that it wasn't possible, that...*one night*. There had been that one night, months ago. Before the contract. Before he'd proposed. Before they'd gotten married.

Maybe this had been her plan all along, to lure him in and have a child, just like countless women had done to rich men in the past. Maybe she'd played him right from that first night. Maybe she was no better than the first woman who'd scorned him.

Damn it! They'd had an agreement, a contract, and he'd be darned if he was going to let her walk out on that and have a baby. A baby that he'd have no choice but to support, to see, to know. A baby he didn't want. A baby that shouldn't even exist. The one thing in life he'd been certain about for the past decade was that he didn't want a woman in his life and he didn't want a family. Ever. The one and only time he'd slipped up, put his trust in someone else...

Blake poured himself another nip, swallowing it

down fast before pushing the glass away. He'd had enough, needed to keep his head, to stay in control.

Saffron might be able to run, but he wasn't going to let her hide. Not with his baby on board. Not now, and not ever.

He sat in silence, in the dark. She was supposed to be dancing again, or had that been a lie? She was supposed to be in contention for a role that she'd seemed excited about. Or was that just a ruse to throw him off track, not make him suspicious?

Blake picked up his phone and scrolled through some numbers until he found the contact from the art auction. It was late but he didn't care—he'd make a donation large enough to make it count. If he found her friend Claire, he'd find Saffron. And if that didn't work, then he'd start at NYC Ballet. He'd contact the airlines, stop her from flying, do whatever it took. She wasn't leaving him—not with his baby.

CHAPTER TEN

SAFFRON HAD NEVER felt so guilty in her life. The pain was shooting through her chest, making it hard to breathe. But the problem was that guilt wasn't the only thing she was feeling.

Her heart was broken. Saffy gripped her water glass tighter, staring at the slice of lemon floating as she sat at the bar in the hotel. Just like every time she started to doubt herself, she touched her stomach, ran her palm lightly across it, just enough so that she hoped the baby could feel.

She checked the time and stood up, ready to take her taxi to Newark airport. It had been a long night, lying awake, wondering if she was doing the right thing, but she'd made up her mind and it was time to go. Maysville, Kentucky, wasn't New York, but it was an amazing place to raise a child and she had her family there. She could start a dance studio one day, nurture young talent, incorporate what she loved with being a mother. Or at least that was what she was telling herself to deal with the move.

"You're my little blessing," she murmured as she walked, one hand carrying her bag, the other on her belly still.

She wasn't supposed to have a baby, and the fact that she'd gotten pregnant was a miracle. A miracle that she had no intention of turning her back on. Dancing had been her everything, until her body let her down. Now her body was doing what it was never supposed to do. It might have been a shock, but she could sure see the irony of it.

Saffron spoke to the concierge as she passed through the lobby and was directed to her taxi, getting in and letting them take care of her luggage. She didn't have a lot, just two suitcases. It seemed ironic that after so many years living in New York, she had so little to take home with her. But her mom would be there to welcome her with open arms, even though they hadn't seen each other in a long time. They were like that—could just pick up where they'd left off. Same with her dad. They knew she loved them and vice versa; she'd just spent so many years doing her own thing that they weren't the best at staying in touch.

She rested her head against the window, the cool glass refreshing against her hot skin. The city whizzed past once they'd gotten through the worst of the traffic, and when they finally reached the airport, she almost couldn't open her door. Leaving New York had never been part of her ten-year plan.

"Ma'am," the driver said, looking back over his shoulder.

Saffy smiled and forced a shaky hand up, opened the door and got out. He was nice enough to help her out with her bags, and she paid him the fare plus a decent tip. Then she went in, checked in for her flight and kept only her carry-on bag in her hand. She knew there would be a long wait ahead of her to get through security, so she went to get a coffee first. When she was finally in line, her hands began to shake, and she clutched the takeout cup tighter even though it was starting to burn her palm.

The line moved slowly, and the anxiety she'd started to feel in the taxi compounded so fast she could hardly breathe. What was she doing? How could she leave New York? She should be dancing for Pierre, she should be back as a principal, her leg was better... Saffy took a slow, steady sip of coffee in an attempt to calm herself.

She was having a baby, and that was the most important thing in the world. She was going to be a mother. She was going to have a gorgeous little child to hold in her arms and love. She could go back to ballet.

Couldn't she?

"Saffron!"

Saffy almost dropped the cup. What the...was she hearing things?

"Saffron!"

Saffy turned slowly, sure she was imagining the deep, commanding voice calling out her name above the din of the airport, the noise and bustle of the busy terminal. She was going crazy, actually crazy.

Blake? *Oh my god*, it *was* Blake! Her heart started to pound. Should she push to the front of the line? Get through security and away from him, beg to be let through? She knew that was stupid—Blake was worth a small fortune, and he'd just buy a ticket no matter what the price so he could follow her.

Saffron held her head high, not losing her place in the line as she defiantly met his gaze despite wanting to cower as he glared. She'd done her best to run away and not have to deal with him, to face a confrontation, but he'd found her and she couldn't back down. It had been cowardly of her to leave him a note, but it had seemed like the only way to break free from him.

"You're not getting on that plane."

Saffy gulped. She guessed they weren't exchanging pleasantries. "I'm going home, Blake, and you can't stop me."

His gaze was cool. Unrecognizable. "Oh, yes, I can. You're not abducting my child, Saffron. Not now, not ever."

She didn't know what to say. It was his child, but she'd expected him to want her to abort, to…maybe he still did, and he was just trying to take charge any way he could.

"I'm keeping this baby, Blake," she said, hand to her stomach, not caring who heard.

"You're coming with me. Now," Blake said, reaching for her, hand closing around her arm and holding tight.

"My luggage is already checked and my flight leaves in two hours."

"Saffron, you're not getting on that plane."

Blake might have been angry before, but now he was furious.

"Let go of me," she hissed, tears welling in her eyes, her resolve fading fast, no longer feeling brave. "You can't just make me."

He didn't look like a man about to take no for an answer. "Sweetheart, we're leaving this airport together whether you like it or not."

She gasped when he pulled her, not letting go. She thought about screaming for security, yelling for help, but the people waiting behind her just looked away, not caring for someone else's problems. Saffron let herself be pulled, wished she was stronger or more determined, but the fight was gone. Extinguished as if it had never existed. Blake would have found her no matter where she was—she'd been kidding herself to think she could run and that he'd forget all about her.

"You can let go of me now," she huffed, pulling back and forcing him to slow down. Blake was impatient, but he did slow, his fingers not gripping her quite so tightly. "And in case you care, you're hurting me."

Blake let go completely then, his hand falling to her back instead, pointing her toward the exit. "Just come with me."

"What about my things?"

"I don't care about your things right now!"

She stopped walking, glared at him. "We're getting my luggage or you can go to hell."

He stared at her for a long moment before marching her back over toward a counter, keeping hold of her as he spoke to someone, flashing a card that she guessed showed he was a priority flyer or something.

"I'm having your things sent. Come on."

Saffron chose to believe him, and within minutes they were seated in a sleek black car, the driver taking off the moment they were buckled in.

"You can't just take me hostage," she managed, forcing the words out as they choked in her throat.

"For the next six months or however long I need to, that's exactly what I intend on doing."

She turned to face him, stared into the eyes that belonged to a stranger right now. Not the handsome, beautiful man she'd slowly fallen for since the night she'd met him. The man she'd been so scared of getting close to, of letting see how broken she was, only to find out that he was broken in just as many ways. Except right now she saw no breaks, not even a crack, just a man calmly and almost silently controlled. This was the first time she'd glimpsed what she presumed was soldier Blake—calm, cool and in control. There was a coolness that was just...*empty.*

"So you want me to have the baby?"

He looked away. "Yes. You can leave as soon as it's born if you like."

"I will not!"

He stared at her, but she wasn't backing down. Not when it came to her baby, and she sure wasn't going to be separated from her child, no matter how much money he had to throw around!

"You used me for my money," he muttered. "You got pregnant, fooled me with your stories of your career aspirations, made me believe that you couldn't ever have a baby. Fool me once, Saffron, shame on you. Fool me twice, and you'll wish you hadn't. I just can't believe I let you close, believed that you were different."

She gulped. "Blake, I'm not going to give you my baby. That's ludicrous!"

"What, you'd prefer just to take my money and raise it alone?" He glared at her. "Not going to happen. You've already done more than enough of that. We're talking about a child here."

"I didn't do this for your money, Blake! You want to investigate me, then go for it. Contact my oncologist, I still have his number in my phone. See my notes, figure out for yourself what a miracle this is that I'm even carrying a child right now," Saffron snapped at him, her confidence seeping back, not about to let him push her around, not now. "No one, not even you, Blake, can act like I haven't worked my butt off for what I've achieved. And that was supposed to be my life, my everything." She fought the tears, wanted to stay strong. "I haven't lied to you, I haven't tricked you, I haven't done anything other than try to deal with this baby on my own so you didn't have to. You've made it more than clear that you don't want a family, and I'm going to make sure my baby feels loved."

He was still just staring at her. "Are you finished?"

She turned away, not about to get into a staring competition. "You can think what you want about me, Blake. But you're wrong."

They didn't speak for the rest of the journey. Saffron wanted so desperately to cry, to just give up, but she couldn't. For the first time since she'd set her mind on being a professional dancer, she had a burning desire within her that no one could dampen. She was going to protect her baby, and no one was going to stand in the way of her being an amazing mom. She might not have wanted to get pregnant; she might not be sure how on earth she was going to do it or what the future held. Except that she had a little baby on the way who needed her more than anything else. Everybody needed a person, and she was her baby's person.

She only wished she had a person herself, someone to look out for her and love her unconditionally.

CHAPTER ELEVEN

SAFFRON HAD HIDDEN in the spare room for as long as she could, but it was starting to feel like being left in isolation in the most desolate of prison wards. Besides, if she stayed hidden any longer, she'd probably die of starvation. The little person growing inside her was demanding food all the time—she could hardly keep up.

"Morning," Saffron said as she forced herself to walk through the living space.

Blake looked up from where he was sitting at the dining table, his laptop in front of him and paperwork sprawled. He didn't say a word, just gave her an emotionless kind of stare.

She opened the fridge with a shaky hand, summoning all her strength, not about to let him bully her. She at least wanted to look strong and in control when he was watching her.

"You can't keep me here like a prisoner," she said, continuing what she was doing so she didn't have to look at him.

He ignored her. She hated the silent treatment, would rather he just yell at her and be done with it.

Saffron felt her body temperature rising, just a slow pooling of heat that started deep in her belly and rose slowly up until it flooded her face. She took a deep breath, trying not to explode.

"How dare you," she whispered, forcing her voice as loud as she could make it. "How dare you treat me like some sort of possession, as if you can tell me what to do?"

"You're not leaving, Saffron. That's all there is to it."

"You jerk," she cursed, fingers digging into the counter for support, not scared to stare at him now.

He finally showed something, let her see a flash of anger as he glared at her. "You signed the contract, remember? You were only too happy to live that life, to take my money, hang off my arm and play the doting wife." He sighed loudly. "And let's not forget about that diamond that used to live on your finger."

She swallowed, refusing to cry, to let him see that he'd hurt her. Who was this man? Where was the man she'd fallen for? Who for a moment in time she thought might have felt the same way she did. How had he disappeared so quickly?

"You told me the ring was mine," she choked out.

"And you told me that you didn't need it," he said, voice cold. "Or have you forgotten that already?"

She took her left hand off the counter, her thumb rubbing over the spot where the diamond had once sat. For months, it had been in permanent residence there, fooling her into a sense of…what? Love? She'd never once thought that he'd actually loved her, but she sure had thought she meant something to him. That it hadn't all been make-believe to him. She'd thought they'd leave their fake relationship as friends, maybe even lovers still.

"You know what? You need to leave, give me some space." She was feeling exhausted, didn't have the will or want to fight with Blake.

"And let you just walk out the door? Not a chance."

Hands on hips, she faced him. "I'm not going to run off, Blake, not now that you know. But I do need you to treat me like an actual person instead of some sort of convict."

He pushed back in his seat, eyes on her. "You expect me to believe that you won't run as soon as I turn my back?"

She glared at him. "I'm not going to run." Saffron shrugged. "You know what? Take my wallet so I don't have any money or identification. Is that enough to convince you I won't run?"

Saffron walked out, moving as fast as she could. She only just made it, not even having time to slam the bathroom door shut before she was doubled over the toilet, throwing up so violently she ended up slumped on the floor after. She wriggled down, put her cheek to the cool tiles on the floor.

"Saffron, are you okay?" Blake's deep voice echoed out from the bedroom.

He could probably see her, but she didn't care, didn't have the strength to rise or even look up. The pregnancy was taking everything from her, draining her, making her so ill she could hardly stand it, and the added stress with Blake wasn't helping.

"Go away," she muttered.

There was no other noise, no other words, and she shut her eyes, wishing for sleep but knowing that what she really needed right now was food. Something small and plain to settle her stomach, to give her the strength to face the day. To face Blake.

A door banged shut and still she didn't move, just lay there, wishing things were different, wishing he hadn't found her. Or maybe she should have just faced him, been honest in the first place.

She'd seen the laughter in their eyes, the way they'd enjoyed her pain. She'd been in love, and he'd been sleeping with more women than she could count.

Don't cry. She'd chanted those two words all day, every day. The other dancers were like hyenas, smelling out tears like a predator smelled blood, and she wouldn't give them the satisfaction. They hated her because she was too young, because she'd gotten the lead role too fast, but she didn't care.

"Sticks and stones," she'd muttered, holding her head high, pretending she just didn't care.

But the truth was that Raf's infidelity had almost killed her, because it had drained her of every bit of energy, every bit of confidence she'd had. But she'd survived it, and then she'd never trusted another man again, surrounded herself with a careful little group of friends she could count on.

Blake wasn't going to be the end of her. Blake wasn't going to take anything from her. Blake wasn't going to have the chance to make her feel the way Raf had back then, because she wouldn't let him.

The door banged again, and she forced herself to rise, one foot after another. She splashed water on her face, stared at her reflection in the mirror before braving the living room again. All she needed was something to eat, and she could go hide in bed again, take a long, never-ending shower.

"I put some things on the counter for you," Blake said, zipping his laptop into its Louis Vuitton case as she walked out. "Decaf coffee, a croissant and a bagel. I figured you'd want something."

Saffron could barely hide her surprise. "Thanks."

"Don't even think about leaving," he said, giving her a hard-to-read look. "Just don't."

And with that he was gone, disappearing into his bedroom for a moment before heading out the door.

The apartment was silent, the only noise the barely there hum of the city outside. Saffron took a look inside the bags, the smell sweet but her stomach tender still. She plucked at a piece of croissant, the delicate pastry still warm and tasting like heaven as it dissolved in her mouth.

She hated him. And she loved him.

How could he be so cool one moment then so thoughtful the next? Or maybe he just felt sorry for her. Or maybe she'd honest to God hurt him so bad he couldn't forgive her. For the sake of their unborn child, she sure hoped not.

Blake stayed at work longer than he should have, but it was easier than going home. His assistant had long since packed up and turned everything off except the two matching lamps in his office that were bathing the room in light.

He'd so far fielded calls from his mother wanting them to go out to dinner with her and postponed a business meeting that was supposed to take him out of town, and he was already exhausted with the lies. His life had once been so simple, so easy. He'd worked alongside men he could trust with his life. He'd flown Apaches and extracted teams from live danger areas. His life had been a mixture of adrenaline and fun and passion. And now he was living a life he'd never imagined, a life he'd thought he'd left behind for good. And having to lie about his fake wife who'd thrown him a curveball. He'd been stupid to think a relationship could be anything other than personal, to think he could have lived with a woman like Saffron without getting close, giving part of himself that he'd sworn never to give again. She'd hurt him just when he'd thought he couldn't be hurt by anyone ever again.

Blake poured himself a small shot of whiskey and downed it, wishing the burn of liquor did more for him rather than just temporarily stun his senses. Marrying Saffron was supposed to have made his life easier, supposed to have helped him, given him some breathing space workwise, solved his problems. After a short reprieve, now all it had done was make what was already an existence he didn't want, worse.

What he needed was to fly again, to get up into the sky and see the clouds and feel weightless. To be the rebel he wanted to be, rather than the perfect son forced to conform. His family meant so much to him; he wanted to care for them and provide for them, but to do that he'd sacrificed his soul. Made a deal with the devil that was his father.

Blake collected his coat and flicked off the lamps. On his way home he collected takeout, choosing Italian since he knew Saffron liked it. He had no idea how he felt about her, what he wanted from her. All he knew was that she was carrying his baby, and that meant he couldn't just kick her to the curb. And he didn't want to.

Saffron had driven him crazy, made him believe in people again, and then she'd gone and betrayed him. Just like Bianca had. Just like his father had.

He steeled his jaw and let himself up to the apartment. At first it took a minute for his eyes to adjust; the lights were on low with lamps illuminating the room. Music played softly from somewhere.

Blake was about to flick the main lights back on, had his hand raised, when he saw her. Saffron had her back to him, arms raised above her head as she stretched then leaped, reaching up, doing something that looked impossible to him on pointed toes before spinning.

He was transfixed, couldn't take his eyes off her.

She dropped forward at the waist, seemed to fall effortlessly down before sweeping back up again and moving side to side. Blake never moved, didn't alert her to the fact he was standing there gaping at her. Because he'd never seen her dance before, and now all he wanted was to watch.

And then she spun in an incredible circle, and he knew he'd been spotted.

"Blake!"

She was breathing heavily, staring at him, eyes wide. It was obvious she'd had no idea he'd been standing there.

"I, ah—" He cleared his throat. "I have dinner. You looked great."

Saffron shrugged, and he noticed how her hand fled protectively to her stomach and stayed there.

"I can't move like I used to, but at least I'm not collapsing into a heap anymore."

Blake set down the food on the table and went to get some utensils and plates.

"You're still wanting to dance?" he asked, wishing he hadn't just asked outright the second the words came out of his mouth. It wasn't exactly something she could just decide to go back to with her stomach rapidly expanding.

"As opposed to having this baby?" she asked, hands on hips.

He hadn't expected her to be so defensive, so protective. She was already like a mama bear, and he admired it, even if he didn't trust her. He liked the flicker of a flame within her, was why he'd been so drawn to her from the beginning.

"You obviously want it," he said, cringing again. For a guy who didn't want to say the wrong thing, he was doing a darn fine job of it. "I just..." He didn't bother trying to finish his sentence or dig himself an even bigger hole.

Saffron blew out a breath, stretching her long limbs out. Her legs were slim but muscled in the way only a dancer's could be, and he dragged his eyes from her. She was beautiful—that was a given even if he didn't like her anymore. Even if he didn't trust her, didn't want her in his bed, didn't... Who was he kidding? He still wanted her in his bed, only he wanted to yell at her and get everything that was weighing him down off his chest first.

"Yes, I want this baby, Blake. It's the only thing in this world I'm certain about right now." She sat down at the table, opening a container and looking in as he watched. "That and the fact that I'm guaranteed to be doubled over that toilet again at least once before morning, because what I seem to have is all-day sickness. The whole *morning* sickness thing is a lie."

Blake didn't know what to say to her, so he just sat, opening another container and waiting for her to have her first choice. She picked spaghetti Bolognese and he chose the linguine, twirling it around his fork as soon as he'd served himself, beyond hungry. Besides, eating meant he didn't have to make conversation and that he could keep his anger in check. Ever since he'd read Saffron's note it had been bubbling, always on the point of boiling over, and being around her only made it worse. He always stayed in control, was used to remaining calm in the worst situations when he'd been a soldier, but nothing had prepared him for dealing with Saffron.

"Are you worse in the mornings?" Blake asked, setting down his fork.

She looked up at him. "So long as I eat early enough I usually make it through the day. Why?"

He wasn't sure it was the best suggestion, but he was drowning here. With Saffron, without flying, with his mind such a jumble of thoughts he couldn't piece together, he was seriously starting to lose it.

"I want to take you somewhere."

She had a look on her face that told him she no longer trusted his suggestions. "What kind of somewhere?"

"Flying," he told her. "I know we've had a rough—well, whatever we've had has been difficult. But I want you to come flying with me tomorrow. In a helicopter."

If she was shocked she didn't show it. "Fine."

Blake was happy to leave it at that while it felt like a win.

"Have you told anyone?" he asked.

"About the baby?" Saffron was watching him, a forkful of spaghetti hovering in her hand.

When he nodded, she took a visibly big breath. "No. Up until you found out, it was just me and the doctor."

He was pleased to hear that she'd at least seen a doctor, that it wasn't just a home test. Although from how sick she'd been, it wasn't likely to be a mistake. And seeing her dancing, the way she'd touched her stomach...despite the fact that she still looked the same physically, she had looked so instinctively pregnant that he knew without a doubt it was true.

"Saffron, this is a difficult question, but..." He pushed back in his seat, knowing she was going to explode, that he would ruin the sense of calm they were finally experiencing. "You're certain it's mine?"

He'd expected anger, but he hadn't expected the torrent of fury that hit him like a power wave.

"Are you kidding me?" Her words were so low, so quiet, but they hit a mighty punch. She rose, palms flat to the table, leaning forward as she stood, staring him down. "How dare you ask me that?"

When he rose her eyes flashed with such a powerful anger that he should have known to back down rather than try to placate her. Blake reached for her, wanting to tell her that he'd needed to ask, to hear her say it, but the moment he approached her—

"Saffron!" He cursed as her palm made contact with his cheek. It took all his strength not to react, to steel his jaw. But he did grab her wrist; he wasn't about to let her get a swing in again.

"Don't you ever ask me that question again, Blake. Never." She yanked her arm, hard enough to make him release it, her glare like venom.

"It was a fair question," he muttered, annoyed now.

"For an idiot," she snapped.

"Come on, Saffron!" Blake laughed bitterly.

"It was a legitimate question! You're asking me to be a father, to parent a child that you know is yours, and I have no idea if..."

"Stop right there," she yelled back. "I never asked you to be a father, Blake. I wanted to give you an out, to raise this child on my own without anything from you, because I knew you didn't want a baby. I wanted to give my child all the love in the world, and I didn't want to back you into a corner, to force you to be someone you didn't want to be."

He sucked in a big lungful of air, calmed down, lowered his voice. "Why? Why give me an out? Why not make me step up? Make me at least reach into my pocket? Isn't that what you wanted?" He shook his head. "Or was that diamond ring enough money for you?" Blake knew it had been a low blow, but she'd pushed him over the edge and he wanted to hurt her the way she'd hurt him. The pain she'd caused him was real, had pushed him into behaving like someone he wasn't. He knew he was being an idiot, but he couldn't help it.

Saffron had tears swimming in her eyes now, but she didn't back down. Looked so stoic, refusing to show any weakness in front of him, and he had to admire her for that.

"You want the ring back?" she asked, staring at him as she reached into her pocket. "Here it is, Blake. Have it."

She threw it at him and it landed at his feet. He never picked it up, just looked back at her.

"You didn't sell it?"

Saffron laughed, but it was a sad, morose sound. "Maybe it meant more to me than you realized."

She left him in the room alone, with a solitaire in front of his booted feet and a table full of half-eaten Italian.

Blake fisted his hands, clenched his jaw tight and refused to react. He wasn't about to trash his apartment just because he could no longer keep his anger in check.

He bent to collect the ring and stared down at it, remembered the laughter and happiness of that day. Even though it had been a contractual agreement, not love, they'd still had fun. And Blake knew that the way he felt about Saffron wasn't…

He slipped the ring in his back pocket and sat back down at the table.

Betrayal wasn't something he was used to feeling, but he knew there was only one reason it had hit him so hard. Because he felt differently about Saffron. Because he cared about her. Because the feelings he had for her weren't anything to do with a business arrangement.

And that's why what she'd done had hurt so badly.

CHAPTER TWELVE

BLAKE HAD HALF expected Saffron to stay in her room all morning, but when he stepped out of the shower, he heard music playing and knew she was already up. He dressed and headed out, checking his watch for the time. It was a perfect, clear day, and he wanted to get up in the air as soon as they could to make the most of having the chopper for the day. It wasn't often they had one grounded unless it was waiting for maintenance, and he'd instructed his team to keep this one that way even if an urgent booking came through.

"Good morning," he called out.

Saffron was fiddling with her iPod and the music died. She was wearing the same outfit he'd found her in when he'd arrived home the night before, tight black leggings and a skintight top. He wanted to glance at her stomach, see if he could glimpse a hint of roundness there, but she gave him a frosty stare and he changed his mind.

"Are we still going up?"

Blake nodded. Living with Saffron and having so much dislike and distrust between them was like being back in his family home when his mom had been giving his dad the silent treatment. Blake had never asked, but he was certain his father had been unfaithful, knew deep down that was the reason behind why the light in his mother's eyes had slowly faded during his teenage years.

"I don't want it to be like this between us," Blake said.

"Says the man holding me hostage and treating me like a criminal," Saffron said, walking away from him.

He didn't bother answering, let her go and listened to the shower when she turned it on. A quick glance around told him she'd already had breakfast, or at least something to eat. Blake thought about ordering up something for himself but changed his mind. He'd collect some food and coffee on their way past to take up for the day.

Spending the day out with Saffron might not have been his best idea, but they were stuck together regardless of what he wanted, and he was ready to man up and deal with it. Even if catching feral cats sounded a whole lot easier than dealing with Saffron right now.

Saffron forced a smile as she stared at the helicopter in front of her. As a dancer, she was used to plastering on a smile and making herself look happy even when she wasn't. And if she was going to survive Blake, she needed to start thinking positively and acting as if she was happy—maybe one day she'd trick her own brain. She had no idea how long she was going to be stuck with him if he became intent on staying in control where their baby was concerned.

"All set?" Blake asked.

She thought about all the times they'd pretended together—that they were a happy couple, that everything was great between them. Saffron knew why that had worked, though, why it had seemed so natural and easy. She'd loved his company, liked the man he was and everything he believed in. And because they'd both entered into their arrangement with eyes wide-open, everything had seemed transparent.

"Let's do this."

She'd never been up in a helicopter, and her legs were a little wobbly at the thought of being so high in the air. Up front. With Blake as her pilot. Saffron gulped.

"You okay?"

She nodded. "Uh-huh."

"For what it's worth, I'm sorry about last night."

She brushed his apology off, not wanting to engage. The last thing she wanted was to argue with him before they went up in the air, and she wasn't ready to forgive him yet, wasn't sure when she'd ever be.

She followed his lead, keeping her head ducked down even though the rotors were still stationary. She'd been reading up about helicopter safety on her iPhone overnight, so she was fully briefed and didn't have to keep asking Blake questions.

Once they were seated, he leaned over her and helped to buckle her in. She held her breath, glanced away, but when she looked back he was still fumbling, his hand grazing her stomach.

"Sorry," he mumbled.

Saffron instinctively sat back, pulled away from him. "It's fine." Once, she'd loved any excuse to touch him and liked whenever he'd touched her. She still *wanted* to want it, but she doubted it could ever be like that again.

"I've done that a hundred times for other passengers. This is crazy." He finally snapped her safely in and sat back, doing his own safety restraints.

Saffron sat back and listened to the helicopter fire into life. He passed her a headset to wear, and when they were finally rising into the air, she clutched her seat as the ground receded below.

"How you doing, rookie?" he asked, grinning across at her.

Saffron forgot all about the ground disappearing below them when Blake flashed her his big smile. She hadn't seen a smile light up his face like that since before they'd gone out to their last cocktail party, the night she'd ended up in the restroom and found out she was pregnant.

His burst of happiness hit her like a jolt, reminding her of why she'd liked him so much, why she'd wanted to stay with him and why she'd been so afraid of hurting him. Of breaking his trust.

As he expertly maneuvered the chopper, she stared at him, unable to tear her eyes away. He was happy. Genuinely, one hundred percent happy. And it showed her a different side to him.

"You're different when you're flying," she said, still watching him.

He looked at her. "How's that?"

"Everything about you," she told him. "Even when you're just sitting, there's a bit of a smile hovering, there's a lightness in your eyes. You're just..." Saffron frowned. "Different. I can't explain it."

He was looking straight ahead now, and she admired his strong, chiseled jaw, the handsome side profile. She might not like the way he'd treated her, but deep down she got it, understood why he was so hurt by what she'd done. She only wished he'd trusted her enough after spending three months with her as his wife, instead of labeling her a gold digger without at least giving her a chance to explain properly.

"That's because this is the first time you've

seen the real me," Blake said, not moving a muscle, staring straight ahead.

Saffron turned away, stared out the window, where everything started to blur a little as they moved fast through the sky. She'd been nervous about going up, but now the helicopter ride was the last thing on her mind.

"Why did you give it up?" she asked. "How could you give what you love up like that? You had a choice, didn't you?"

Blake never answered her, and she never asked again.

They'd been up in the air for what felt like forever, but Saffy still hadn't had enough time to think. She doubted she ever would, not when it came to Blake. Something about him made her crazy, made her feel things she was scared of and had thought would never happen to her.

"Descending," Blake said, loud and clear through the headset.

He hadn't spoken a word to her since just after

takeoff, and Saffron felt a weird kind of divide between them. There was so much she wanted to ask him, wanted to say. Only nothing felt right when she sounded it out in her head first.

They landed in a field, a ranch from what she could see, and Saffron stayed quiet as Blake did his thing. When he slipped his headset off, she did the same, watching as he exited the helicopter and then opened her door and held up his hand to help her out.

Saffron took it, letting him guide her down. She stretched, taking a look around.

"Let's go," Blake said.

"Where?"

"For a walk over there." He pointed. "We can have lunch under that tree."

Saffron didn't question him, just followed, staying a step or two behind him and looking at their surroundings.

"Where are we?" she asked when he stopped under a pretty oak tree, its branches waving down low and shielding them from the intense sunshine.

"My family used to own this ranch," Blake said. "It was somewhere we came over the summer or just for a weekend getaway. My best childhood memories were spent here."

Saffron listened as she continued to look around. She touched the trunk of the tree, ran her fingers across its gnarled bark. There were indentations in it, markings that she couldn't quite figure out.

"That's me," Blake said, standing close behind her. She could feel his breath, the warmth of his big body as it cast a deeper shadow over her, making her own body hum even though she tried so darn hard to fight it.

"You?" she managed.

"Yeah." He leaned past her, his arm skimming hers as he traced his fingers across the same spot hers had just trailed over. "I etched my name in here a few times. I used to ride out here on a cute little pony who was always happy

to go as fast as I wanted, and when I got older
I landed my first solo here."

Saffron was aware of everything, could fee
his body even though he was no longer touching her, her breath loud in her own ears, hear
thumping. There was nothing she could do to
stop the way she reacted to him.

"My dad saw how much I loved it here, knew
how much pleasure I got from flying out here
practicing everything I learned."

"He didn't want that?"

Blake made a grunting noise, and she knew
he was stepping away. It gave her breathing
space, but she liked having him near, wanted
him to stay closer.

"It was around the time we'd started to but
heads a lot. All the time," Blake said. Saffron
turned and saw him hit the ground, his big
frame sprawled out. He had one leg out straight
the other bent, resting on one arm as the other
plucked at a strand of grass. "I started to talk
about what I wanted to do with my life, and

that didn't tally up with what he wanted. He went from loving my interest in helicopters to despising it, because every time I went up in the air it made me more determined to carve my own path."

Saffron sat down, leaning against the trunk she'd been studying. "I'm sorry."

He laughed and raised an eyebrow. "What for?"

"I'm sorry that you had a dad who couldn't support your dreams. That he had a hold on you that you still haven't been able to shake."

Blake's stare hardened. "I lost that hold, Saffron. I lost it for years, but in the end it was a hidden choke hold that I'd never truly escaped. It started back then, tightened when he paid Bianca off to leave me and then again when he died."

"You need more of this. To remind yourself of what you love."

If she'd been his wife, his real wife, it would be what she'd insist on.

"Anyway, why am I telling you all that stuff?"

She wasn't buying his laugh, knew it was no joke to him. "Because you wanted me to see the real you," Saffron said quietly. "You wanted to show me who you really are."

"You sound so sure about that." Blake opened a bag and pulled out a couple of Cokes, holding one out for her.

"Can I ask you something?" Saffron said, her heart starting its rapid beat again, near thudding from her chest.

"Shoot."

"Did you ever feel anything for me? I mean, anything real?"

Blake had the Coke halfway to his mouth, but he slowly lowered it. "Did you?"

"I asked you first," she insisted, wishing she hadn't asked him but needing, *craving*, the answer.

"You mean did I want you in my bed? Did I want you at my side, on my arm?"

She sucked in a breath. "I know you wanted

me in your bed—that's the only thing I'm sure about. But..." Saffron paused. "Was the way we looked at each other real? The way we..."

This time when her voice trailed off she didn't bother to finish her sentence. What was she trying to say?

"Whatever we had was just part of a deal," Blake said matter-of-factly. "Was I attracted to you? Of course. Any hot-blooded man would have been. But we didn't have anything more than sex and a contract."

Saffron had tears burning in her eyes like acid, making her want to scream in pain. But she stayed silent, swallowed them down. She'd thought the feeling had been reciprocated, that he'd felt something real for her, like she had for him, but she'd been wrong.

"Why, did you expect something else?" he asked.

Saffron bravely shook her head. "No. I was just curious." Sobs racked her body, jarred her ribs and her shoulders and every other part of her. But she kept her chin up, sucked back silent gasps to stop herself from giving in, from letting him see how much he could hurt her. *Just like dancing*, she told herself. Crying over real pain, over a real injury, was one thing, but that was the only thing any dancer would ever shed a tear over.

"Do you have anything to eat in there?" she asked instead, desperate to change the subject.

Blake nodded. "Sure. You hungry?"

Saffron nodded. She'd rather eat than talk any more.

Blake had shown her his true colors, how happy he could be in the air, what made his heart sing. Only she'd expected, *hoped*, that there would be more. That he'd say something else, tell her that he felt something, *anything*, for her.

Because even though he'd hurt her and she'd tried to run back home, what she felt for Blake was real. It always had been. She'd slowly started to fall in love with him, a man so beautiful yet damaged by a father and an ex-lover who had done him more harm than good, and a career that he'd loved yet one that had shattered parts of him emotionally, as well.

But that man wasn't hers to take, wasn't hers to love. She was having his baby, and that was it. He didn't love her back—maybe he didn't even care for her beyond what she meant to him on paper.

And that hurt so bad it made her injury seem like a cakewalk.

She touched her hand to her stomach, something she was doing instinctively all the time now. If it wasn't for the baby, she'd be long gone now, and Blake would be a distant memory. *Or would he?*

Maybe without the baby everything would have stayed the same. They'd still be living in their little faux bubble of a marriage.

"Sandwich?" Blake asked, leaning forward and passing it over.

"Sure," she murmured, not bothering to ask what was in it. She didn't care.

"You sure you're okay? You're feeling all right?" Blake asked.

Saffron forced a smile. "I'm fine. Thanks for bringing me here."

"You're the first person I've ever flown out here," he said, taking another sandwich out and holding it in his hands, watching her.

"I thought…" She didn't know what she'd thought. Did that mean something—was it supposed to mean something?

"I want our baby to start flying young," Blake said, surprising her with his smile. "It's all I ever wanted, and if I'm going to share it with anyone, who better than my child?"

Of course. It was the baby. That was the only reason he'd brought her. She'd been fooling herself that maybe he wanted to talk to her, to get away from the city with her for a reason, but now it was all about the baby.

So much for him not wanting to be a dad.

"We need to figure this out, how it's going to work," Saffron said, not seeing any point in putting it off. "You don't have to do this, playing the dad role. It was my choice to keep the baby, and I'm okay with that."

The happy lilt of Blake's mouth disappeared, replaced with a much tighter line. "Oh, yeah? So I could just write a card on birthdays or maybe just Christmas."

Saffron refused to take the bait, didn't want to end up arguing with him when she had no chance of winning.

"What I'm trying to say is that I want custody. I don't want to fight about it, but a child needs to be with its mom," she said, bravely meeting his gaze head-on and refusing to shrink away from him. "You'll always be welcome, I'm not trying to tell you to stay away, I'm just saying that…"

"Oh, I hear what you're saying," Blake muttered. "You're laying it on pretty thick."

"Blake! You don't even want this child! You

don't want to be a dad!" Saffron didn't know how to keep her cool, what to say. He was driving her crazy. "We're not a real couple. There is no way for this to work."

Blake stood and stared down at her, his shadow imposing. "I wasn't under any illusion there."

He stormed off, and she didn't bother calling out. She wasn't about to follow him, either. Instead she sat there, picking at her sandwich even though the last thing she felt like was eating.

How had her life turned out like this? She was sitting here all high and mighty about how much she wanted this baby, and she did, but she wasn't *actually* ready to be a mother. All she wanted was to be back on stage, back dancing. Saying yes to performing at Pierre's retirement party. And instead she was growing a big round belly and thinking about names and genders and how on earth she was going to provide for the little future love of her life.

Saffron bit hard on her lower lip. Everything

was a mess. She didn't want Blake and his money, but if he didn't let her go back home, then she'd have no other choice but to take whatever he offered. But if he even for a second wanted to take her child from her, take control... She pushed the thoughts away. It wouldn't come to that, because she wouldn't let it.

Suddenly Blake was storming back in her direction, his face like thunder. As she watched, he gathered everything up and marched it back to the helicopter. Saffron stood and reluctantly followed—it wasn't as if she had an alternate ride home.

"We're going," he said.

She shook her head. "Why can't we stay? I think you should blow off some steam before..."

He spun around, only a few feet from her, his hands clenched at his sides, his anger palpable.

"You know why I brought you here?" he asked.

Saffron stayed still, stared at the bulge in his

neck where a vein was about to pop out from under his skin.

"I thought we could start fresh, put the past behind us. I brought you here because this place means something to me, and I wanted to show it to you." He ran a hand through his hair, anger still radiating from every part of him. "I wanted to see if you actually cared about me, whether we could at least agree on something to do with this child, *our* child."

"I do care about you, Blake," she said softly, telling him the truth. "You're the one who just acted like what we had meant nothing, that it wasn't real."

"Yeah? You care about *me*?" He laughed, but it sounded forced. "Well, you've got a real strange way of showing it."

"Blake…" she started. He'd just been the one saying there was nothing real between them, yet now suddenly everything was her fault!

"Get in the helicopter, Saffron," he demanded

as he spun back around. "Or find your own way back to the city."

She wanted to believe that he wouldn't actually leave her behind, but given his mood, she wasn't sure about anything right now.

"I'm sorry," she said as she followed him.

"Yeah, me, too," he muttered back.

Saffron took his hand to guide her into her seat, but she never looked at him when he settled beside her and started to flick switches, the engine humming into life. Things had gone from worse to bad to worse again, and there was nothing she could do to change it.

CHAPTER THIRTEEN

THEY'D BEEN SILENT since the ranch. Saffron had
goose pimples rippling across her skin whenever she looked at him, but still they never ut-
tered a word. They'd landed, he'd helped her
out, driven her home, and now he was about to
head out the door for takeout. She knew this because he'd phoned and ordered Thai, and she'd
been sitting in the same room as him, snuggled under a mohair blanket while he'd been
positioned at the dining table furiously banging
away at his keyboard. She was half expecting
him to need a new machine in the morning the
way he'd been treating it.

"I'll be back soon," Blake said.

When she looked up, he was standing near

the door, his eyes still shining with anger. Or at least she was guessing that's what it was.

"Okay." Saffron forced a smile, but he was still staring at her and his gaze was unnerving.

"That's it. That's all you've got to say to me?" His voice was so low, so quiet it was lethal.

Saffron gulped, wished she knew the right thing to say. But the truth was that she'd tried to run from a man with trust issues, and she had no idea what to say to make that situation better.

"I'm sorry. I'm sorry for what I did, Blake, I am," Saffron said, forcing the words out. "But I'm not sorry for what happened, because it's nothing short of a miracle, no matter how scary it is."

He went to turn and she breathed a sigh of relief, but he hadn't moved his body halfway to the door when he was staring at her again. He didn't say anything, just stared, but she could feel the unsaid words hanging between them, knew he was bottling a whole heap of something inside.

"Why can't you just accept that what happened was an innocent mistake? That I never…" She didn't bother finishing. They'd been through all this—there were only so many times she could apologize for what she'd done.

"You want to know why?"

Blake's words sent shivers through her. She was scared of the way he felt, of what he made her feel. The way she felt about him, despite everything.

"Why?" she whispered as he spun around to face her. She'd asked; it wasn't as though she could walk away from him now.

"Because I loved you." He hurled the words at her, and she instantly felt their sting. "I lied before, okay? I fell for you because I thought you were different. I was stupid enough to think that what we had meant more than…"

"Some stupid contract?" she said for him, finding her voice. "I didn't hear you ever offering to rip that up. Not once, during all the times we connected, when I felt like we were something more, did you *ever* make out like you wanted to make what we had real."

It was unfair—she'd agreed to their marriage bargain right from the start to help her stay in New York, but he was hurting her and it was all she had. Because she *had* felt the same, had thought she was falling for him, that something between them was real. That it wasn't all just about their stupid agreement.

"Why didn't you tell me," she finally said when he never spoke. "Why didn't you say something, *anything*? Why couldn't you have just done something to show me?"

"What difference would it have made?" Blake asked, his tone cold, blunt. "What would it have changed between us?"

It would have changed everything. Saffron squared her shoulders. "It would have made a difference," she said, knowing in her heart that it would have. That if she'd just known for sure that he felt about her the same way she was feeling about him…

"What, you would have felt bad about using me? About lying to me?" He laughed. "Would it have changed how guilty you're feeling right now?"

"No," she said simply, tears threatening to spill even though she was trying so hard to fight them. "Because then I would have known that my own feelings were real, that you didn't just think of me like..."

"Like what, Saffron?" he bellowed. "I've treated you with nothing but respect and kindness! I treated you like my real wife, didn't I?"

"I was in love with you, too!" she sobbed. "How could you not have realized how I felt? How could you have been so blind?" Saffron turned away then, couldn't look at him any longer. She was still in love with him, despite everything, and it broke her heart to argue the way they were. "All you had to do was say something, Blake. Instead you hid behind your daddy issues, kept acting like you could never be the man you were so good at pretending to be with me." She shook her head. "You kept saying you couldn't settle down, couldn't ever be a real husband, but in the almost four months I spent with you, I saw a man who could have had whatever he wanted. A man who could have been a darn good *real* husband if he'd wanted to be. You didn't exactly make it look hard."

He stared at her, but she was on a roll now, couldn't stop.

"You're hiding behind your past, not letting yourself live, because you're too scared of change, of what might happen, of being hurt and exposing yourself to that kind of real love. I'm not judging you—heaven knows I'm no different—but things have changed, Blake. Things changed between us long before I took a positive pregnancy test."

"Just go," he finally said, his voice hoarse, unrecognizable. "If you want to go back home to raise our baby that bad, just go."

She hated the emptiness to his tone, the hollowness. It was the same way she felt inside, like a soft toy with all the stuffing knocked from her. "After all that effort to keep me, now you're going to just give up without a fight?" Saffy knew she was being antagonistic, but it was true.

"What do you want from me, Saffron?" he whispered, eyes level with her own.

"I want you to want me, Blake!" she told him, voice shaking. "I want you to fight for me. Show me that I'm not just some asset to you."

"You want me to fight for you?" he muttered, marching toward her, stopping barely an inch away, towering over her, his body almost brushing hers, his gaze fierce. "Consider me in the ring then."

Just as she was about to reply, about to stand her ground, Blake's hand cupped the back of her head, the other snaking around her waist. He pulled her forward, dropped his mouth over hers and kissed her as if it was the final kiss of their lives.

"Stop," she protested, hands to his chest, half-heartedly pushing him away.

Blake didn't let up, kept kissing her. "This is me fighting," he said against her lips. "You want to go, you pull back."

Saffron tried—she wanted to push him away completely. She wanted to forget about him and get on with her life without him, but she couldn't. Because from the moment they'd met, something had ignited between them that she hadn't wanted to admit, and that spark was far from being extinguished. And he'd just told her that he'd loved her. Admitted that what she'd felt between them had been real.

"We can't do this," she whispered, finally parting her mouth from his, dropping her head to his chest, letting him cradle her as she absorbed the warmth from his body.

"You're my wife," he murmured, lips to the top of her head, soft against her hair. "We can do anything we like."

Saffron wanted to give in, wanted to believe

him, but… "I can't. We can't." She shook her head, palms to his chest again, forcing some distance between them, needing to look up at him. "We need to talk. Actually talk. Not yell at each other, or make assumptions. I need to talk, and you need to listen. We can't just bury our heads in the sand. Not this time, Blake."

Blake took Saffron's hand and led her to the sofa, sitting down and waiting for her to do the same. He felt as if he'd just stepped off a roller coaster; his body was exhausted and his mind was a jumble. The past few days hadn't exactly been easy, had drained everything from him. And now he had to dig deep and not push his feelings away like he'd been doing for most of his adult life.

"So let's talk."

Her smile was shy as he watched her, and he sat back, glanced away, hoping to make her feel more comfortable. All he'd done since he'd hauled her back from the airport was to tell her what he thought, bully her, throw his weight around. And that wasn't him, wasn't the man he wanted to be. It was the man his father had been. The kind of cold, unfeeling, calculating man his father had shown himself to be time and time again.

Which was exactly why he'd never wanted to be in this position, to be a dad or a husband. Blake pushed the thoughts away, focused on Saffron. Whether he wanted to be a dad or not was irrelevant now, because he was going to become one regardless. What she'd said had hit home, was true even though he didn't want to admit it. He had been hiding behind his past, living his life with a raft of excuses about what he couldn't do. And that needed to end now. If he wanted to step up and be a parent, not lose the woman who'd finally made him feel, then he needed to be a man.

"I never lied to you, Blake, and we can't move forward unless you believe that."

He nodded. "If I wasn't starting to believe

that, we wouldn't be having this conversation." Blake wanted to blame her, but she didn't deserve it.

He watched as she blinked, staring down at her hands. There should be a ring on her finger, a ring to show every other man in the world that she was taken. Their relationship might have been fake to start with, but he was only kidding himself that he didn't want her as his, and he wanted it clear to every man alive that she wasn't available. Suddenly the fact that there wasn't a ring sitting against her skin made him furious.

"I'm scared of being a mom, of holding this baby when it's born and trying to figure out what to do with it, but for the first time I can remember, I want something as bad as I want to dance." She sighed. "And that scares me as much as it excites me."

Blake reached for her hand, squeezed it when he saw a trickle of tears make their way down her cheeks. If she'd wanted to show him what an idiot he'd been, she was doing a fine job. There was no way he could feel worse about his behavior if he tried.

"I'm sorry," he said, clearing his throat, wanting to do better, knowing it might be his only chance after what he'd said. "I'm sorry, Saffron. If I could take back half the things I've said to you, I would."

She nodded, eyes shut as she took a big, shuddery breath. "I want to dance so bad, but I also want this baby, Blake," she said. "I can't explain it, but it's so powerful, so instinctive."

Blake brushed the tears away with his knuckles when she opened her eyes, gentle as he touched her skin. He got how hard it was to open up and be honest, and she looked as though it was hurting her real bad to say how she felt.

"I've been an idiot," he said, finally getting the words off his chest. "I don't exactly find it easy to trust, but you didn't deserve the way I treated you. You deserve an apology."

"You're right," she said, "but I should have

told you instead of running away. I made myself look guilty of the crime—you just put the pieces together. And you're not the only one who's said things they regret."

"Why?" he asked. "I still don't understand why you decided to run. I'm not going to lose the plot about it again, but you need to explain it. I need to be on the same page as you, Saffron. Why did you run?"

Her eyes filled with fresh tears as he stared into them, but this time he didn't brush them away, didn't try to comfort her. This time he just needed to listen, and she looked as if she was ready to talk.

"I was terrified you wouldn't want the baby," she whispered, no longer meeting his gaze. "That you wouldn't want anything to do with our child, and I didn't want this baby to feel unwanted."

"What?" He held her hand tighter, fought the anger as it started to bubble within him again. Blake waited a second, not wanting to overreact, needing to calm down before he spoke. He'd wanted her to be honest, and she was, which meant he couldn't judge her for her thoughts. But still, keeping a lid on the way he was feeling wasn't easy.

"I know how strongly you feel about not having a family. How determined you were *not* to be a father, to not ever be put in that position. Not to let your heart be broken by a woman, too."

He took a slow breath, not wanting to snap her head off. "I would never, ever not want my child to be born. And I'd never make a child feel unwanted. Not my own flesh and blood. *Never.*"

"But…"

"I'm terrified of the idea of being a dad, knowing that there is a baby coming into this world with half my DNA," Blake continued, needing to get it all off his chest before it strangled him. "I don't want to be a dad because I had a terrible example from my own father, and I don't want to become that kind of man. To have a child of mine feel such hatred toward me that the moment he finds out his own father has died he feels a sense of relief."

Blake stood, turned away, gulped away an emotion that he'd never let out before. Something he always extinguished long before it threatened to surface.

"Blake?"

Saffron's hand was on his back, her touch light, her voice kind. But he didn't want her to see him lose it like this, break down when he was usually so strong, so incapable of anything getting under his skin.

"Just give me a sec," he muttered.

"You can't help the way you feel," Saffron whispered, her hand snaking around his waist, slowly, turning him toward her. "Whatever you felt when he died, it's okay. You can't keep all that bottled inside."

Blake shut his eyes, squeezed the tears away. He was not going to cry, not in front of Saffron. Not ever. Tears over anything other than an atrocity weren't for men who'd seen terrifying things, seen what he'd seen when he was serving. There was no way he was shedding tears, not now, not ever. Not over some stupid feelings he'd had for his father.

He opened his eyes and stared into dark eyes that seemed to see straight into his soul. Blake opened his mouth, wanted to tell her she was wrong, but instead a wave of guilt, of emotion and sadness and regret, hit him like a tidal wave. A gulp of tears burst out, the emotion flooring him, his knees buckling as everything he'd held back came pouring from him.

"Shh," he heard Saffron murmur as she held him, cradling his head to her stomach as he stayed on his knees, felled like an oak tree slain at the heart of its trunk in front of her. "Shh."

Her hands were warm, her touch so gentle, but Blake couldn't stop, the sobs racking his body as the pain slowly washed over him. He didn't try to speak, couldn't get anything out except the grief he'd held so tight for so long.

"Tell me," she said. "Get it all out. You need to share it with someone. Just say the words."

Blake steadied his breathing, felt the rise and fall of Saffron's stomach against his cheek. He had no idea what had come over him, but he couldn't believe what he'd just done. And then he shut his eyes again, tears no longer engulfing him.

His baby was in there. Saffron had been holding him, comforting him, and he hadn't even realized how close he'd been to his little unborn child. It gave Blake the strength to rise and face her again, this woman who'd turned his life upside down and made him feel things, move forward instead of just treading water. If he was going to be a dad, he needed to be honest with himself. And with Saffron.

"I hated him," Blake finally said, keeping hold of her hand and drawing her back onto the sofa with him, keeping her in his arms so he could cradle her warm body against his. "I saw so much while I was serving, realized I was actually living the life I was supposed to live, making a difference in the world and flying the machines that made me feel so amazing. The only stumbling block in my life was my father. And the woman who'd hurt me, made me feel stupid and vulnerable in a way that only my dad had been able to do before."

"Did he ever accept what you did?" she asked, head to his chest. "Ever give you praise for the career you'd made for yourself?"

Blake didn't want to look at her, just wanted to touch, to feel her there with him. It made it easier for him to say the words he'd only ever said in his head before.

"I grew up around helicopters and planes, and I loved it. I guess that's why Dad thought I was a natural fit for the company, or maybe it was just because I was his firstborn that he felt that way. Before I started to fly myself, at the ranch, I was trailing around after him at the hangars, checking out our stock and soaking up every word he or anyone else in the know said about them. It probably never crossed his mind that I wouldn't do what he wanted me to do."

"But you loved actually flying more than the company, right?"

Blake dropped a kiss into her hair, craving her, suddenly needing to stay connected after so long spent trying to push her away.

"I was addicted to flying from my first flight, and I was a natural in a helicopter, just like I told you today. After he sent my fiancée running for the hills with a pocket full of cash, I knew I had to get away. I hated him so much, and I found my place in the world. I had an amazing job in an industry that needed me, I got to fly every day and I had a new family with my army buddies."

Blake paused, thought back to how he'd felt the day his dad had passed. "He never supported my dreams or wanted to hear anything about my life, not unless I went to work for him. He didn't want to hear about the lives I'd saved, the men I'd flown into dangerous situations to help protect our country that he claimed to love so much. And he sure didn't want to hear about how bad it affected me, that half the time I couldn't sleep for weeks after I returned from a tour."

"You can't help that you hated him, Blake. We feel what we feel, and there's nothing we can do about it," she said.

"Things just got worse and worse, until I couldn't even stand being in the same room as him. Not even at Thanksgiving or Christmas, and I know it broke my mom's heart, which was something I never wanted to do."

Saffron was stroking his shoulder, her face to his chest as she listened to him.

"I have nightmares about what I saw when I was serving, dreams that will haunt me forever, but I'm the type of person who's okay with that because I want to know the realities of our world. I don't want to live in a bubble where rich people have everything and don't care about the world or real people or the next generation." He blew out a breath, amazed how fast the words were falling from his mouth now that he'd started talking, how desperate he suddenly was to share them. "When I heard his helicopter had gone down, that he was presumed dead, it was like a lead weight had been lifted from my chest, a weight I hadn't even known was there. It was a feeling I'll never forget for as long as I live."

Blake stayed silent for a moment, regretted the thoughts he was having, hated the pain he felt at what came next.

"And then I found out that my brother had been flying with him. That it wasn't just my dad, but my brother, too," he murmured. "In that one second, I wished so bad that it was all a mistake, felt so guilty that I'd been relieved about Dad disappearing off the face of the planet."

"You were close to your brother?"

Blake nodded. "My brother was my best friend growing up. We were so different and we fought like crazy sometimes, but I loved him. I'd do anything to have him back, would have traded anything and everything to change places with him and be on the chopper that day. I still would."

"You can't think like that," Saffron said, pushing back and looking up at him. "That's one thing you just can't let yourself think."

"Yeah, I can," he grumbled. "He was with my dad that day for work. If I hadn't been so pig-headed about making my own way in the world, it would have been me with him flying out to meet a new corporate client, not my brother. It would have been me missing, and he'd still be here."

Saffron didn't say anything, just kept stroking his shoulder, her fingers running lightly across his T-shirt.

"It should have been me," he whispered.

"But it wasn't, and I'm glad," Saffron said,

her voice soft yet fierce at the same time. "Because then I would never have met you, and we wouldn't have a little baby on the way. This little baby that is an absolute miracle."

Blake touched her stomach, laid his hand flat there, the first time he'd done it, and it calmed him. Made him feel a crazy mix of emotions, protective over the tiny being he'd helped to create that was cradled in her belly.

"I'm scared," he admitted.

"Me, too," she whispered back. "But you're not your father, and I'll never let you turn into him. This baby is going to be whatever he or she wants to be. All we have to do is love and nurture and care for this little person. It's all he or she will need."

"You sound so sure." Blake looked down at her, realizing how stupid he'd been to have almost let her go. She'd been so close to just slipping from his life.

"Being in love and loving is the only thing I am sure about right now."

And just like that, it was Saffron with tears in her eyes and him wanting to be strong for her, and everything else fell away except the woman in his arms.

CHAPTER FOURTEEN

"SO WHAT ARE we going to do?" Saffron asked, closing her eyes and enjoying the sensation of Blake strumming his fingertip across her skin. She snuggled in closer to him, the sheets covering their lower halves, their uppers bare.

"Not much more of that," Blake said with a chuckle. "It can't be good for the baby."

She laughed. "It's fine for the baby. I checked with the doctor."

"I'm glad to hear you had your priorities straight when you were asking questions about our unborn child!" Blake flicked her, his touch no longer so soft and lingering.

Saffron pushed up on her elbows, looking down on Blake. "I'm serious. What *are* we going to do?"

"We're going to get married. For real this time," Blake said, pushing up and pressing a kiss to her lips, his smile serene, a peacefulness on his face that she hadn't seen before. "No registry office this time around."

She giggled when he tickled her. "I can't exactly wear white. I think the tummy will give away my virtue, or lack of."

Blake pulled her closer, rolling them over until she was pinned beneath him, his arms imprisoning her on each side.

"I can't promise that I'm going to be a good dad, but I'm going to try my hardest," Blake said, staring into her eyes. "I don't want to be my father. I don't want to ever be that kind of man, but I want this baby." She smiled, seeing the emotion on his face, the tears welling in his eyes that mirrored hers. "And I want you."

She slipped her arms out and slung them around his neck, needing to hold him, to pull him closer. "I love you, Blake," she whispered.

He dropped a soft, gentle kiss to her lips. "I love you, too."

Saffron smiled so hard, she couldn't have wiped it from her mouth if she'd tried. "I didn't think I'd ever hear you say that. Not to me, not to anyone."

He held her tighter, sighing against her skin. "Me neither, sweetheart. But then I never expected to come across a woman like you. The gloves are off, Saffron. I'm all yours."

"All mine," she murmured as he planted a full kiss to her lips. "And don't you forget it."

EPILOGUE

BLAKE COULDN'T TAKE his eyes off Saffron. *His wife.* His cheeks were sore from smiling so hard, watching as she somehow floated across the stage, twirling and leaping and…he had no idea what any of the moves she was doing were, but whatever it was, she looked incredible. Seeing her like this reminded him again of what he'd been so close to losing, how stubborn he'd been about the only woman who'd ever managed to see the real him.

"Mama."

He glanced down at the little girl sitting in his lap, clapping her pudgy little hands at least every other minute. She'd wriggled to start with, but from the moment her mom had graced the stage, she'd been transfixed, quiet as a mouse as she sat on his knee in the front row.

"Yes, Mama," Blake whispered back to her. "Isn't she amazing?"

"Mama," Isabella said again, clapping and tipping her head back so she was resting against him as she looked up.

Blake focused on Saffron again as she did something else incredible before stopping, her feet no longer moving, her pose perfect as the lights slowly went out. Within minutes the lights were rising again, flooding the theater at the same time that Saffron stood in the center of the stage, the crowd bursting into applause. Then she was joined by the other dancers, but Blake only had eyes for his wife, unable to drag his gaze away for even a second.

He couldn't believe how much she'd changed him, how different he felt from the man he'd been only a few years ago. He held Isabella tight, loving every second of having his little daughter close. She was the best thing that had ever happened to him, even if he was fiercely protective of her, so in love with her that it hurt sometimes.

"Go see Mama," Isabella demanded, wriggling so hard he could barely keep hold of her.

"Come on, let's go then," Blake said, scooping her up in one arm and holding her against his chest. She tapped his head.

"Sho-sho," she said, smiling up at him. Blake never had a chance of saying no to her, not when she looked the spitting image of her mother with her beautiful dark eyes, deepest red hair and angelic smile.

He lifted her up onto his shoulders, which was what she'd been asking for in her own little language, chuckling to himself about the fact he had a tutu all ruffled around the back of his neck. She was just like her mom when it came to ballet, too, and very opinionated about what she liked to wear. Tonight she'd wanted to look like a real ballerina, but she wasn't a pink girl, so it was a dark blue outfit with a tutu and matching shoes covered in bling and she looked impossibly cute.

"Mama!" Isabella squealed when she spotted her mother.

"Hey!" Saffron came running, her face alive as it always was when she was on a high after a performance. Blake hadn't seen her dance live in a show until Isabella was a year old, and now he hated to miss seeing her on stage. Although his daughter was very opinionated about being left home with a sitter, preferring to snuggle up in their bed.

"You were amazing," Blake said, pulling her tight into his arms for a quick kiss before he was pushed out of the way by his daughter, who now only had eyes for her mother.

"Hey, beautiful! Did you enjoy it?" Saffron asked her.

Isabella tucked her face against her mom's chest for a moment before pushing back and touching her mom's cheeks and then patting her hair. Saffron's hair was almost always down

when she was home, but when she was performing, it was always pulled up tighter off her face
and Isabella seemed transfixed with it.

"You know, if we were normal people, we'd
have her with a sitter so we could go out for
a late dinner," Blake said, laughing because
he knew exactly what kind of reaction he was
going to get from his wife.

"Wash your mouth out!" Saffron scolded,
pulling Isabella's head tight to her chest and
covering one of her ears. It was a constant joke
between them, and even though Blake suggested it regularly, they both preferred to take
Isabella out with them whenever they could.
Especially now that Saffron was back dancing
and he was so busy with the company during
the day—they juggled as best they could, but
after hours they liked to be a tight family unit.
Unless his mother begged to have her grand-
daughter to stay, which usually resulted in a
little girl packing her suitcase immediately and
demanding to go.

"How about a quick ice cream on the way home instead?" Blake asked, reaching for his daughter and pulling her off Saffron.

"Yay!" Isabella squealed.

Saffron nodded. "Sounds good. Just let me change and say goodbye to everyone."

Blake waited for his wife, chuckling to himself how much his life had changed. Meeting Saffron had changed everything, made him realize how lucky he was in so many ways.

"You know, I took your mommy out for ice cream when I first met her."

"Mommy love ice cream," Isabella said, patting his arm, her beautiful dark eyes looking tired. Not that his daughter would admit to being sleepy for a second, though.

"Mommy was so beautiful then she took my breath away, and she still does," Blake replied without a hint of a lie. "I was a fool once, but when I found out you were in Mommy's tummy, I stopped being so stupid. I asked her to marry me."

"Tell me, story, Daddy."

"What story?" Saffron asked, slipping her arms around him from behind.

Blake grabbed her with his free hand, snaking it around her and pulling her close.

"I'm just telling Bella about when we were first together. Every time we're alone and you're dancing, I tell her how I fell in love with you when she was just a little button in your tummy."

"Oh, really?" Saffron said with a laugh, one eyebrow arched.

Blake laughed and dropped a lingering kiss to her lips when she tilted her head back to stare up at him.

"Really," he replied.

They left the building snuggled up tight, his daughter still in his arms and his wife tucked to his side. They'd never once told another soul the truth about their marriage, how they'd met and the marriage contract they'd once signed. Saffron had even managed to convince her friend Claire that they'd been secretly dating before their fake marriage. Only Blake's lawyer knew the truth, and he paid him enough not to breach attorney-client privilege.

"Our little secret, huh?" Saffron whispered in his ear.

Blake grinned and held her tighter. "Yes, Mrs. Goldsmith," he teased.

He had it all, and nothing would ever be more important to him than caring for his family, fiercely protecting them and doing everything in his power to be everything his father hadn't been.

He'd spent all his life terrified of becoming that man, and in the end nothing could be further from the truth. From the moment he'd accepted how much he loved Saffron, to seeing his newborn daughter in his arms, he'd known there was no way he could turn into him. Not for a second.

"I love you," she murmured, head to his shoulder.

"I love 'cream," Isabella mumbled in a sleepy voice.

Blake grinned. "And I love Mama *and* ice cream."

They walked out the back exit to avoid any lingering fans, heading for their favorite ice cream parlor. The night air was cool, and he tucked Isabella closer against his chest and Saffron even snugger under his arm, loving the warmth of them.

"Surprise!"

Saffron laughed as her husband stopped midstride, eyes wide as he stared around the room. She ran over to him, throwing her arms around him. He gave her a glare that turned to a sigh and then a smile.

"You fooled me," he muttered.

She shrugged. "Yep, I did."

Saffron had told him it was a simple birthday celebration, just the three of them having dinner with his mother, and instead she'd filled their home with everyone he cared about, including some of his friends and former colleagues that she knew he'd been sorely missing.

"You're crazy," Blake said, holding her tight and kissing her hair.

"It's not only me who gets to live my dream."

He raised an eyebrow and she bit down on her lower lip, watching as his old buddies engulfed him, slapping backs and giving friendly hugs. She'd seen the pain he'd been in at giving that life up, and he'd made her dreams a reality by helping her every step of the way. Not to mention getting a whole lot of flak for rescheduling his days when she was performing to be a stay-at-home dad. It was a role he loved, but she knew it wasn't exactly easy for a company CEO to take time off when all his peers had nannies.

"Saffron, you've got some explaining to do," Blake called out, pushing his friends away and holding out a hand to her, tugging her over.

She couldn't hide her smile, knowing what he was about to say.

"What kind of wife organizes a boys' helicopter weekend for her husband?"

Saffron winked at him, something he often did to her, and it made him chuckle.

"You might not be able to fly for the military again, but it doesn't mean you can't fly with at least some of your old team," she said, standing on tiptoes to kiss him, wanting him to have an amazing birthday. "It's only camping, but I figured it was the closest to replicating what you used to love. There's no use owning a fleet of planes and helicopters if you can't use them, right?"

His smile was impossibly charming, his eyes dancing as he gazed down at her. "You know what I do love right now?"

She tipped her head back. "What would that be?"

Blake swept her up in his arms, lifting her high-heeled feet off the ground and kissing her in front of everyone. His friends clapped and catcalled, but Saffron didn't care that they were putting on a show for them.

"You."

"Just so happens," she said, nipping his bottom lip when he tried to kiss her again, "that I feel the exact same way."

* * * * *